W9-BEO-630

"Boy, am I glad to finally meet you two!"

Wishbone trotted closer to the two German shepherds. "You must be Iggy and Axel. I'm—"

"Grrrrrr!"

The German shepherds dropped the rubber bone and bared their teeth at him.

"That's not quite the greeting I was expecting, guys."

"Grrrrrr!"

"Wow—" replied Wishbone.

Before Wishbone could finish, both German shepherds lunged at him. Wishbone yelped and scooted backward—just in time. The dogs' teeth clamped down on the air right next to his tail.

"Hey! I happen to be very attached to my tail—and I'd like to keep it that way!" Wishbone said.

As Wishbone quickly sized up the situation, the two dogs came at him again, barking and growling.

"Yikes!" Wishbone sent dirt flying as he turned and ran, with Iggy and Axel right behind him. "Time for a strategic withdrawal. In other words . . . I am outta here!"

WISHBONE™ ***Mysteries***
titles in Large-Print Editions:

#1 *The Treasure of Skeleton Reef*

#2 *The Haunted Clubhouse*

#3 *Riddle of the Wayward Books*

#4 *Tale of the Missing Mascot*

#5 *The Stolen Trophy*

#6 *The Maltese Dog*

#7 *Drive-In of Doom*

#8 *Key to the Golden Dog*

#9 *Case of the On-Line Alien*

#10 *The Disappearing Dinosaurs*

by Anne Capeci

WISHBONE™ created by Rick Duffield

Gareth Stevens Publishing
MILWAUKEE

This book is a work of fiction. The characters, incidents, and dialogues are products of the author's imagination and are not to be construed as real. Any resemblance to actual events or persons, living or dead, is entirely coincidental.

For a free color catalog describing Gareth Stevens' list of high-quality books and multimedia programs, call 1-800-542-2595 (USA) or 1-800-461-9120 (Canada). Gareth Stevens Publishing's Fax: (414) 225-0377.

Library of Congress Cataloging-in-Publication Data

Capeci, Anne.
Key to the golden dog / by Anne Capeci; [interior illustrations by Don Adair].
p. cm.
Previously published: Allen, Texas; Big Red Chair Books, © 1998. (The Wishbone mysteries; #8)
Summary: When the valuable steam engine from an antique model railroad system vanishes during Oakdale History Month, Wishbone and his friends try to unravel the mystery of its disappearance.
ISBN 0-8368-2389-3 (lib. bdg.)
[1. Dogs—Fiction. 2. Mystery and detective stories.] I. Adair, Don, ill. II. Title. III. Series: Wishbone mysteries; #8.
PZ7.C17363Ke 1999
[Fic]—dc21 99-20013

This edition first published in 1999 by
Gareth Stevens Publishing
1555 North RiverCenter Drive, Suite 201
Milwaukee, Wisconsin 53212 USA

Edited by Pam Pollack
Copy edited by Jonathon Brodman
Cover concept and design by Lyle Miller
Interior illustrations by Don Adair
Wishbone photograph by Carol Kaelson

Printed in the United States of America

1 2 3 4 5 6 7 8 9 03 02 01 00 99

For Delphine

FROM THE BIG RED CHAIR . . .
Oh . . . hi! Wishbone here. You caught me right in the middle of some of my favorite things—books. Let me welcome you to the WISHBONE MYSTERIES. In each story, I help my human friends solve a puzzling mystery. In *KEY TO THE GOLDEN DOG*, Sam and I look into the disappearance of the model engine from an antique railway set, on display in Pepper Pete's Pizza Parlor.
The story takes place in the spring, during the same time period as the events you'll see in the second season of my WISHBONE television show. In this story, Joe is fourteen, and he and his friends are in the eighth grade. Like me, they are always ready for adventure . . . and a good mystery.
You're in for a real treat, so pull up a chair and a snack and sink your teeth into *KEY TO THE GOLDEN DOG*!

Chapter One

Samantha Kepler smiled to herself as she skated in circles on the pavement outside Sequoyah Middle School on Monday afternoon. The bright sunshine felt warm on her face, and a spring breeze ruffled her blond hair. All around her, young green shoots pushed out from the earth, and new leaves budded on the trees. Everything was so alive and bursting with energy that it made Sam itch to be on the move.

"Come on, guys," she said to her two best friends, Joe Talbot and David Barnes. The boys were sitting on the curb in front of her, putting on their in-line skates. "Let's get going."

"What's the hurry?" Joe asked. As he pushed off from the curb to join Sam, his white-with-brown-and-black-spots Jack Russell terrier, Wishbone, jumped around his feet.

"Do I need a reason? How about blue skies, beautiful warm weather . . ." Sam stopped to scratch Wishbone behind his brown-spotted ears. "*And* the model train that's going on display later this afternoon at my dad's restaurant."

"Hey, I almost forgot about that," said David, strapping on his safety helmet. "It's part of Oakdale History Month, right?"

Sam nodded. The Oakdale Historical Society sponsored a celebration of the town's past every April—complete with special events. This year the society had something even better than usual to display, and Sam couldn't wait to see it.

"It's an antique model-train set that includes the stores, the houses, and farms . . . everything. It re-creates Oakdale and this whole area during the early 1900s," she explained. "I haven't seen it yet, but Miss Gilmore told my dad it looks like a real town."

Wanda Gilmore was president of the Oakdale Historical Society, as well as the Talbots' next-door neighbor. She had phoned Sam's father the night before to confirm that she would be bringing a work crew to Pepper Pete's Pizza Parlor the next afternoon to set up the model train. Sam was curious to see it. She already knew a lot about Oakdale's past, but she always enjoyed learning even more.

"Miss Gilmore told my mom about the model train, too," Joe said. "She said it was a miracle that old Mr. Ottinger agreed to put it on display."

"I know." Sam stopped skating so she could pick up a tree branch that had fallen to the pavement. "He *never* gets involved in—"

As she was about to toss the thin branch to Wishbone, the double doors of the school banged open. A girl ran out, carrying a pair of in-line skates in one hand, and her backpack in the other. She had wideset brown eyes, a pale complexion, and wavy black hair that bounced around her shoulders.

"Isabel!" Sam cried out, waving.

Isabel St. Clair had just started at Sequoyah a few weeks earlier, after transferring from her old school in San Francisco, California. Sam didn't know the girl very well yet. But she figured it had to be hard to move someplace new toward the end of the school year. Sam wanted to do what she could to help Isabel feel at home.

"Hi, everybody! What are you up to?" Isabel called back. As she jogged over to Sam and her friends, Isabel seemed very glad to see them. Sam had the feeling Isabel wanted to make friends.

"We're going to Pepper Pete's to check out a hundred-year-old model-train set," said Joe. "Want to come?"

Isabel's smile faded. She glanced uncomfortably down at her skates and mumbled, "Oh . . . a . . . uh . . . m-model train?"

Sam exchanged surprised looks with Joe and David. Just a moment earlier, Isabel had seemed really interested in what they were doing. Why was she now cooling off?

"I guess seeing a model-train set isn't the most exciting thing in the world," David said. "We'll understand if you don't want to come."

"I *do* want to," Isabel said quickly. She smiled, but she still seemed hesitant.

"It should be interesting," Sam told her. "The model-train set is owned by Carl Ottinger. He's this odd man who's lived in Oakdale practically since the town was founded."

"The guy's a living legend," Joe added. "His family was in the railroad business. Mr. Ottinger started working in the family company when he was just a teenager. He made a name for himself when he faced off with some thieves who boarded a train and tried to steal the safe. Mr. Ottinger was outnumbered, but, armed with a pistol, he somehow managed to drive off the robbers."

"After that, *everyone* knew about Mr. Ottinger," David said. "He had a reputation for being tough, smart, and very independent. By the time he was in his twenties, he was practically running the company."

Sam glanced at Isabel. She would have expected some kind of reaction. But Isabel was bent over her skates, an unreadable expression on her face. She didn't say anything. She just slowly fastened each buckle. Sam didn't know what to make of Isabel's behavior—so cheerful and friendly one second, quiet and withdrawn the next.

"Carl Ottinger must be almost ninety by now," Sam said. "Hardly anyone ever sees him, but Miss Gilmore says he's as stubborn and unsociable as ever. She almost didn't believe it when he agreed to display his model railroad for Oakdale History Month. He always ignores town events. But it looks like some relatives talked him into getting involved this time."

"I'm surprised Mr. Ottinger would follow anyone

else's advice," David said. "I've always heard he likes to be the one giving orders. That was true when the golden dog was missing, anyway."

"Golden dog?" Isabel asked, looking up. "What's that?" There was a spark of interest in her eyes, as if she had decided that she wanted to be involved in their conversation once more.

"A gold charm that belongs to the Ottingers. It was shaped like a dog, with emerald eyes," David explained. "There was a lot of excitement about it a long time ago, when it disappeared. Mr. Ottinger was such a powerful man in town, and he raised a huge fuss about it. So now everyone in Oakdale knows the story."

"What happened?" Isabel asked. "How did the charm disappear?"

"No one knows for sure," David told her, "but Mr. Ottinger insisted someone stole it. He had the police running around in circles looking for it. They never found any sign of a break-in, but Mr. Ottinger wouldn't hear of any other explanation."

"What David is leaving out is that the police had a theory of their own," Joe said. "You see, Mr. Ottinger had a young son who really liked to play with the golden dog. The boy drowned at around the same time the golden dog disappeared. Mr. Ottinger was really grief-stricken about his son's death. The police thought he might just have . . . imagined the theft. When they hinted at that, Mr. Ottinger threatened to have every police officer fired. I guess he was powerful enough to do it, because the police kept looking for the dog."

"So the real reason he was upset was because he lost his son," Isabel said, her brown eyes wide. Sam saw that the girl was completely caught up in the story now.

"Wow! The charm must have been doubly important to him because the boy loved it."

"It was also valuable. It had been given to his family by some Chinese royalty," Sam told her. "It was unique—the kind of thing he could never replace."

"One of a kind?" Joe raised an eyebrow at Sam as he skated idly past, with Wishbone running beside him. "Sounds like the diamond in that mystery you told me about, Sam—the one you found at your mom's house."

"*The Moonstone,*" said Sam. She tapped the paperback book that stuck out from her jacket pocket. "An English author named Wilkie Collins wrote it more than a hundred years ago. Mom told me it's considered the first modern detective novel."

Sam hadn't read much of the mystery yet, but already she was hooked. "The story takes place in England, back in the middle of the nineteenth century," she explained. "It's about an unusual yellow diamond called the Moonstone. It was originally part of a shrine in India."

"Sounds unique, all right," said David.

"And valuable," Sam added. "So valuable that a British soldier stationed there stole it."

"Hold it," David interrupted. "I thought you said the story takes place in England. But you just mentioned India."

"That's just background information," Sam told him. "The real story starts when the soldier who stole the diamond decides to give it to his niece, Rachel Verinder, for her eighteenth birthday. The soldier asks a young man named Franklin Blake to take the diamond to Rachel at her family's estate in Yorkshire, in the English countryside. But when Franklin Blake gets there, he thinks he's been followed."

"Really?" said Isabel.

Sam nodded. Glancing at her friends' faces, she saw they were just as curious about the story as Isabel was. Even Wishbone looked interested. "Franklin Blake has heard that three Hindu holy men have dedicated their lives to protecting the Moonstone. He suspects they are the ones following him. Rumor has it that they won't rest until they've recovered the diamond and returned it to the shrine in India."

"Wow," said David. "So Franklin Blake thinks the Hindu holy men are trying to take back the diamond?"

"Yup," Sam answered. "That's all I know so far, but I'll keep you posted after I've read more."

She coasted slowly, letting her imagination wander. She could picture life for the Verinders during the 1850s—a very large country house and huge gardens, with servants everywhere. It was so different from today and Oakdale. The characters in the novel talked and dressed much more formally than people nowadays. But what was most fascinating was the sense of mystery the place had—the feeling that beneath the beautiful surface lay hidden dark secrets. . . .

"What about the golden dog?" Isabel's voice broke into Sam's thoughts. "Was it ever found?"

Sam had been so busy thinking about *The Moonstone,* she'd forgotten about Carl Ottinger and his missing gold charm. Looking back at Isabel, Sam again saw the curiosity in her eyes.

Hmm . . . thought Sam. *Why is Isabel so interested in the golden charm?*

"I don't think the family or the police ever found the charm," Sam answered. "I guess we'll never know what happened to it."

As Isabel got to her feet, Joe skated over, with Wishbone by his side, and scooped up her helmet from the ground. With a smile, he handed it to her and asked, "Ready to roll?"

Isabel's look of interest faded to a frown. "I guess so . . ." she mumbled. Without looking at anyone, she started skating.

There she goes again. Interest one minute, disinterest the next. What is going on? thought Sam.

Letting out a sigh, Sam patted the copy of *The Moonstone* in her jacket pocket. *I guess now I have* two *mysteries to think about,* she thought—*what's going to happen to the Moonstone, and why Isabel is acting so weird.*

"Did someone say 'go'? You don't have to tell me twice." Wishbone kicked up his hind paws and ran down the sidewalk after Joe, Sam, David, and Isabel. "I like to run—especially when there's pizza at the final destination. What about if we try the pepperoni today, okay, Joe?"

The little terrier gave his biggest doggie smile, but Joe didn't seem to notice.

"Uh . . . Joe? I'm talking pizza here! Hellllooo!"

Joe smiled at Isabel. "I've been wondering about something," he said. "What made your family decide to move here?"

Wishbone sighed. "Okay, we'll talk pizza later. If you and Isabel are going to be friends, I guess I'd better find out more about her, too." Perking up his ears, he gazed at Isabel. "You were saying . . . ?"

"We moved here because of my great-grandfather. He's pretty old," Isabel said. "I guess he wants his family around him now, because he called Dad in San Francisco and asked us to move back here."

"Your family is from Oakdale?" Sam asked. "You didn't say anything about that before."

As Wishbone ran along, he looked back and forth at the faces above him. "Are you okay, Sam? Why are you staring at Isabel?"

There was something odd about Isabel, thought Wishbone. While she talked, she looked down at her skates instead of at the person to whom she was speaking. Her behavior seemed familiar to Wishbone, although he couldn't quite put his paw on why.

"We're not from here, really," Isabel said. "My dad grew up in California, and I've kind of lived all over the place. Dad's a civil engineer. We've moved around a lot because of his work. My great-grandfather is the only one of us who's lived in Oakdale his whole life."

Isabel's cheeks suddenly got red. Looking up at her, Wishbone realized exactly what it was about her that was familiar to him. Her actions reminded him of the way he felt when the Talbots' next-door neighbor, Wanda Gilmore, caught him digging in her flowerbeds! She looked guilty.

Wishbone cocked his head to one side to look at Joe's new friend more closely. "But Isabel, why would you feel guilty?"

"Great-grandpa asked us to move back here. And he asked my dad to take over some of his business interests. Mom and Dad said yes," Isabel went on. "Dad says it's a good opportunity to get to know Great-grandpa. He sure could use the help. Before we came to Oakdale, he was all alone in that big old house of his. The only person there to help him out was his housekeeper, Mrs. Hazlett. We now live with him."

"Your great-grandfather must be glad you're here," Joe said.

"I think Great-grandpa's happy about it," Isabel said. "Anyway, I'm glad Mom and Dad and I are around now to keep him company. Iggy and Axel help keep the house lively, too."

"You have brothers?" David said, as he coasted up from behind.

"I guess you could say they're like brothers," Isabel said, smiling. "Except furrier. Iggy and Axel are my dogs, David."

Wishbone gave a joyful bark, letting his tongue wag from his mouth. "As I suspected, a dog lover! Well, that's all I need to know. Joe, did I mention that I approve of Isabel?"

"I've always wanted some animal friends, and when we moved here, my parents finally gave in," Isabel went on. "Iggy and Axel are pretty high-spirited, but they're not even a year old. I guess it's going to take a while to train them."

"I can help with that!" Wishbone smiled up at Joe, his tail wagging. "It looks as if you and I can both make new friends."

Wishbone ran happily the rest of the way to Pepper Pete's. He scooted through the doorway just as Joe opened the door, then paused and sniffed the air.

"Mmm-mmm! The pepperoni smells especially good today, Walter." Wishbone gave a big smile to Sam's father, Walter Kepler, who was busy behind the counter. "There sure are a lot of people here today." He looked eagerly around at the kids who took up most of the restaurant. Joe's mother, Ellen, was also there, along with a few other adults. "This train thing must be special—Ouch!"

Wishbone yelped as something hard poked his nose from above. Looking up, he saw a wooden cane poised just over his head. The handle was in the shape of a dragon's head. Scales were carved down the length of the cane's shaft.

Only after Wishbone had jumped out of the way did he get a look at the man who held the cane. The terrier saw bushy white eyebrows, eyes that were all business, and a hand that looked ready to poke the cane at him again. "A simple 'Excuse me' would do," Wishbone said in an irritated tone.

"Wishbone!" a familiar voice called out.

Wishbone didn't have to look up to know who the voice belonged to. It was Wanda Gilmore, the owner of the flowerbeds where some of Wishbone's best bones were buried. She and Ellen were standing next to the white-haired man, frowning down at Wishbone.

"Wishbone, I don't want you getting into Mr. Ottinger's way," Ellen said.

As soon as he heard the old man's name, Wishbone forgot his annoyance. "Did you say Mr. Ottinger? Joe! Here's that living legend you were just talking about."

Wishbone looked back to see Sam, David, and Joe by the front door of Pepper Pete's. They all stared curiously at Mr. Ottinger while they changed from their skates to sneakers. Only Isabel hung back.

"Hi, Miss Gilmore. Hi, Mrs. Talbot," Sam said, with a smile. "We came to see the model-train display."

"It's actually called a 'model *railway*.' You're just in time for the unveiling," Wanda said. "I'd like you all to meet Mr. Ottinger and his grandson and granddaughter-in-law, Mr. and Mrs. St. Clair. They're the owners of the model railway, and today's guests of honor."

Wishbone sat back on his haunches to look up at the couple standing with Wanda, Ellen, and Mr. Ottinger. "St. Clair? Isn't that Isabel's last name?"

"Now, we're just waiting for the St. Clairs' daughter, Isa——"

"Isabel, there you are!" Mr. St. Clair called out.

Wishbone noticed that Isabel still lingered near the door. "Hi, Dad, Mom. Hi, Great-grandpa," she said. "Sorry I'm late." As she came forward to greet them, she glanced nervously at Sam, David, and Joe.

Wishbone gazed at Isabel in surprise. "You mean, *Mr. Ottinger* is your great-grandfather?"

Chapter Two

Sam stared in amazement as Isabel kissed Mr. Ottinger on the cheek. "Mr. Ottinger is Isabel's great-grandfather!" she whispered to Joe and David. "Why didn't she tell us?"

"Beats me," Joe said, frowning. "She listened to all those stories about him as if it were the first time she'd ever heard of him. Did she think we wouldn't find out Mr. Ottinger is related to her?"

"That's hard to believe," said David. "Isabel had to know her parents and great-grandfather would be here today."

"That's another thing she didn't tell us," Sam said. "She acted as if she didn't know anything about the unveiling of the model train—*railway,* I mean. Isabel was coming here anyway, but she didn't say a word about it."

Sam tried to understand why Isabel would mislead them on purpose. But the only person who could answer that question was Isabel herself.

"I'm going to talk to her," Sam decided.

Pepper Pete's was crowded. Kids headed toward the back of the restaurant, where a work crew was bent over a platform that stretched almost halfway across the back wall. Sam got a tempting glimpse of some model buildings and gleaming railroad tracks that wound through rolling green hills. It looked as if Oakdale had been mostly farms and woods back when the model railroad was made. Sam was eager to take a closer look. But that would have to wait until after she talked to Isabel.

Sam walked back to the entrance, where Isabel stood with her parents, her great-grandfather, Joe's mother, and Miss Gilmore.

"Hi, Sam." Isabel greeted her with a shaky smile. "I'd like you to meet my mom and dad. And this is my great-grandfather."

"Nice to meet you," Sam said. She smiled at everyone. But the person who most captured Sam's attention was Isabel's great-grandfather.

Sam had seen Mr. Ottinger only once or twice in her life. Now that she was right in front of him, she understood why people felt threatened by him. His steely-gray eyes gave you a look into his stubborn side. His tall, wiry body seemed packed with energy. With his bushy eyebrows, thick mane of white hair, and carved-dragon cane, he seemed larger than life.

"Isabel has told us about you, Sam," Mrs. St. Clair said warmly. "It's a pleasure to meet you in person."

Isabel's great-grandfather barely nodded at Sam. "Let's get this over with, before I change my mind," he said sharply to Isabel's parents. He waved his cane at Wanda. "You, there! What's holding things up?"

"The workmen are making some final adjustments, Mr. Ottinger. They'll be just a minute longer," Wanda said, smiling.

"Come see for yourselves," Ellen added.

As Wanda and Ellen led Mr. Ottinger and Isabel's

PEPPER PETE'S

parents toward the platform, Sam held Isabel back. "Can we talk?" Sam asked.

"S-sure," said Isabel.

There were a lot of people standing near the entrance, so Sam led the way to the counter. Joe and David were already standing there, with Wishbone at their feet.

"We're really confused, Isabel," Sam said. "Why didn't you tell us Mr. Ottinger is your great-grandfather?"

Isabel's eyes flicked nervously from face to face. "I'm sorry," she said. "I know I should have told you. It's just that . . . well . . . everyone knows all those stories about Great-grandpa. They make him sound so . . . unfriendly. I guess I thought you might not want to be friends with me if you knew I was related to him."

"Being Mr. Ottinger's great-granddaughter doesn't change the way we think about you," Joe said right away.

"It's kind of cool knowing you're related to someone who's famous around here," David added.

"Really? You don't know what a relief it is to hear that." Isabel let out a sigh, then turned to Sam with an uncertain smile. "So, you're not upset with me?"

Sam still thought it was odd that Isabel had not been upfront with them in the first place. But the look on Isabel's face was so sincere, Sam forgave her right away. "Of course not," she said. "I still can't believe you're related to someone we've heard stories about our whole lives."

"Sometimes it's hard for me to believe, too—especially when I hear things about Great-grandpa that I didn't know before," Isabel said. "I mean, I never heard a thing about the golden-dog charm you mentioned. But I do know some of the other stories. Like the one about Great-grandpa's son. My dad told me about how he died when he was just a boy. He was my grandmother's brother, Will. Dad said Great-grandpa took his death really hard."

"It's understandable," Joe put in.

"It was hard on the rest of the family, too," said Isabel. "Great-grandpa was really difficult to be around after that. My grandmother left home as soon as she was old enough. She met Grandpa St. Clair in San Francisco, and that's where she spent the rest of her life. Grandma Sarah told Dad and me about Great-grandpa whenever we visited her. She never came back to Oakdale, and now it's too late. She died last year."

Sam tried to imagine what it would be like to be out of touch with her dad for so many years. But she couldn't. It was too sad. "Well, at least it's not too late for you," she told Isabel.

"That's what Dad says." Isabel smiled and glanced across Pepper Pete's at her great-grandfather. "Great-grandpa can come across as cold. It's as if he's got this tough shell around him and he won't let you in. I guess it's hard to change after all this time, but we keep hoping he will. That's the main reason Dad and Mom decided to get involved with Oakdale History Month—so we could get closer to Great-grandpa. They thought he would have a lot of Oakdale history to share with everyone, since he's lived here so long."

"No kidding. He's probably a walking history book," David said.

"Hey, I know what you should do, Isabel!" Sam said. "We're doing a special issue of the school newspaper for Oakdale History Month. I'm going to contribute photographs. Why don't you interview your great-grandfather and write an article?"

"I'm not sure he'll want to participate, but . . . well, it would be a good way for me to get to know him better."

Isabel seemed to think it over for a moment. Then she smiled and said, "I'll ask him tonight."

"Great!" said Sam. "There's a meeting about the special issue tomorrow after school. Let's go together."

"Attention, everyone!" Wanda called from the back of Pepper Pete's. "We're about ready for the trial run!"

Sam was glad she and Isabel had cleared the air between them. Her behavior earlier now made sense. Now she couldn't wait to get a look at the model railway and Oakdale's history!

She, David, Joe, and Isabel all pressed toward the back of the pizza parlor. As they approached the platform, Sam peeked over the shoulder of a girl in front of her.

"Wow!" she said enthusiastically.

There on the platform was a panorama of Oakdale. Sam recognized Lake Oakdale, as well as half a dozen buildings along Main Street.

"Look! There's the Oakdale *Chronicle* building!" she exclaimed, pointing. "And isn't that Pepper Pete's?"

Sam's father stepped from behind her and slipped an arm around her shoulders. "It's the same building, but back in those days it was the Oakdale Pharmacy."

David pointed to a shiny, black steam engine that sat on the train tracks with half a dozen passenger and freight cars hitched behind it. There was even a caboose. "The train is amazing. Check out all the details," he said. "The brass bell, the whistle . . . And look inside. Do those levers really work?"

Sam wasn't surprised to see the gleam of interest in David's eyes. He liked everything mechanical.

"You bet," Isabel said proudly. "So do the doors and windows. Pretty incredible, isn't it?"

"Oakdale sure has changed since the early 1900s,"

Sam said. "Back then there were hitching posts instead of parking meters. And farmland where my house is."

"Great-grandpa's house is there," Isabel added, pointing to a model of a large stone house on the outskirts of town. It had three chimneys, and a covered entryway with a model horse and carriage beneath it.

"Mind letting someone else have a look?" A boy's voice spoke up.

Sam turned around to see Damont Jones, one of Joe's basketball teammates. Damont elbowed his way past half a dozen kids, trying to get closer to the platform.

"Take it easy, Damont," Sam said. "Everyone will get a chance to see."

Damont shrugged. He opened his mouth, but before he could say anything, Wanda spoke up.

"Get ready, everyone," Wanda called. "It's show time!"

"Can I see, too?" Wishbone wound his way through a dense forest of legs and feet, trying to get to the model railway. "Make room for the dog, folks!"

He wriggled left, then right, until he reached the front of the crowd. Scooting past Isabel, Wishbone rose up on his hind legs, leaning against the platform for a look.

"There's Main Street, all right!" The terrier's tail wagged excitedly as he smelled oil, metal, wood, and paint. "Hmm . . . my favorite oak tree was just a sapling back then. And there are hardly any cars. I wonder how dogs went on road trips years ago."

He sniffed eagerly at tree-covered hillsides and green-painted fields dotted with wooden cows. "I bet there were a lot more squirrels to chase, but . . . Hey! Where are all the dogs?"

Wishbone looked once, then again. He didn't see a single canine.

Dropping back to the floor, the terrier gazed up with disappointment at Isabel. "On behalf of all the dogs of Oakdale, I want to make a complaint!"

Isabel didn't even glance at him. She was too busy listening to Wanda. Everyone was.

"On behalf of the Oakdale Historical Society," Wanda was saying, "I'd like to thank Mr. Ottinger and the St. Clairs for displaying this invaluable piece of Oakdale's heritage. Mr. Ottinger, would you do us the honor of turning on the railway?"

Isabel's great-grandfather stepped slowly over to the platform. As he passed Wishbone, the dog kept an eye on his cane. "Watch the tail, please."

Mr. Ottinger stopped next to the platform. He flipped the switch and the train jumped forward on the track.

"Here we go!" Wishbone couldn't help running around the table and jumping up for a closer look. The engine rumbled, the whistle sounded, and the metal wheels screeched as they picked up speed. Wishbone's tail thumped wildly back and forth as the train charged through fields, climbed rolling hillsides, sped around curves.

"Down, Wishbone," Joe called. But it was a command Wishbone simply couldn't obey. He barked for joy as the model engine disappeared inside a tunnel. Tongue wagging, he ran to the tunnel's end, then jumped up again.

"Here it comes! Faster than a speeding tennis ball . . ." The model engine shot from the tunnel and flew down a hill, rounding a tight curve. "More powerful than a— Hmm . . . isn't that train going a little *too* fast for that turn?"

All of the sudden, the model train let out a terrible *screeech!* that made Wishbone cover his ears with his paws. The engine's metal wheels jumped the track, with the train still moving at top speed.

"Runaway train! Look out!" Wishbone howled as the engine flew toward the edge of the table—straight toward him!

Chapter Three

"The train . . . It's derailing!" Sam watched in horror as the model engine leaned toward the edge of the platform—where Wishbone was watching the action.

"Wishbone, look out!" Sam called out.

She heard Wishbone's yelp and then saw him dive beneath the platform. A second later, the model engine tipped over the edge of the platform right where his head had been. The engine broke free of the other cars and hit the floor with a crash.

Cries of alarm rang out from the crowd. Sam pushed forward, reaching the model-train set at the same time as Mr. Ottinger, Wanda, Ellen, and Isabel's parents did. The model engine lay on its side on the floor. Wishbone crouched just behind it, carefully sniffing at the overturned metal wheels.

"Are you all right, boy?" Joe asked, as he and Sam crouched down next to the platform.

Upon seeing them, Wishbone stood up on all fours, stretching each paw. Then he wagged his tail, as if to say, "No need to worry, everyone. I'm okay!"

Once Sam was sure he wasn't injured, she turned her

attention to the model engine. She held her breath as Isabel's great-grandfather picked it up. He, Wanda, and Isabel's parents all bent to examine it. A moment later, Mr. St. Clair straightened up and gave the crowd a relieved smile.

"The engine's all right," he announced. "There's not a scratch on it."

"What a relief," said Ellen.

Sam joined in as several customers clapped. "I'm so glad," she said, turning to Isabel, David, and Joe. "I would have felt awful if—"

"Peter, Marla, I thought you told me the railway would be safe here!" Mr. Ottinger glared at Isabel's parents, tapping his wooden cane against the floor to stress his words.

"It is safe, Grandfather," Isabel's father insisted.

"I should have stuck to my guns and steered clear of this nonsense," Mr. Ottinger grumbled. He turned to Wanda. "Have your men take the railway back to my house at once."

"What!" Sam turned to her friends in alarm.

"What's his problem?" Damont muttered, flicking a thumb at the old man.

Sam noticed that Isabel overheard what Damont had said—she looked embarrassed. Her cheeks turned red, and she stared down at the floor. Everyone was watching Mr. Ottinger.

"Damont, Mr. Ottinger is upset. His train engine could have been seriously damaged," Sam said. She knew Damont hadn't meant to upset Isabel. But he had a way of saying the wrong thing at the wrong time.

"Please go on back to your tables, everyone," Sam's father called out. "We'll get the kinks worked out in a minute. Sam, can you help with the orders until things calm down?"

Sam nodded. Following her dad behind the counter, she grabbed an apron and order pad. But her mind was still on Mr. Ottinger. He was surrounded by Isabel's parents, Ellen, and Wanda, next to the model railway. They were all talking to him in hushed tones, but he just kept shaking his head.

"Do you think they'll be able to talk him into leaving the railway on display?" Sam asked her father.

"I hope so," he said. "People enjoy seeing Oakdale's past. And it sure is good for business. Every table is filled, and it isn't even dinner time yet."

"Ridiculous! That's what this Oakdale History Month is!" Isabel's great-grandfather exclaimed. He was talking to Wanda, Joe's mother, and Isabel's parents, but his voice carried through all of Pepper Pete's. Isabel's face turned an even brighter red. She was really embarrassed. Now that Sam saw Mr. Ottinger in action, she could understand why.

"Well," Mr. Ottinger continued, "I won't leave Will's favorite toy here to be ruined because of . . ."

Sam didn't listen to the rest of what he said. "Will?" she echoed. Pulling the apron over her head, she shoved her pad in the pocket and hurried to the booth where Joe, David, and Isabel were sitting. "Isabel, isn't Will the name of your great-uncle? The one who died?"

Isabel nodded. "No wonder Great-grandpa is so worked up about this whole thing. It's because the model railway originally belonged to Will!" she said. "I guess I can understand why he wouldn't want to risk it getting ruined."

"You know . . ." David glanced back at the railway, trying to figure something out. "The only problem was at that downhill curve. I think I could fix it so the train won't derail."

"Really?" said Isabel. "If we can just convince Great-grandpa . . ." She grabbed David's arm and pulled him from the booth. "Come on!"

Sam, Isabel, Joe, and David hurried over to the model railway. Stepping in between her great-grandfather and Wanda, Isabel said, "Great-grandpa, if we can make sure the train runs smoothly, there's no reason to take down the display, right?"

"Isabel?" Mr. Ottinger stared down at her in surprise. "What's this all about?"

"David says he knows how to repair the railway so the engine won't derail," Isabel explained.

Isabel's great-grandfather gave David a slow once-over. His steady, steely-gray eyes seemed to take in every detail of the boy. "My family didn't build up a railroad business by asking strangers for help. I'm not about to start now," he said firmly.

"David isn't a stranger," Isabel insisted. "He's my friend."

"And he certainly knows a lot about building things," Ellen added.

"It would be a simple repair," David said. "All I'd have to do is make a guardrail for that downhill curve. I think that would keep the engine from derailing. I could make it at home tonight and install it before school tomorrow."

The plan was so simple, Sam didn't see how Mr. Ottinger could refuse. Isabel's mother and father looked at each other. "Sounds like a good solution to me," said Mr. St. Clair. "What do you say, Grandfather?"

Isabel and her parents looked expectantly at Mr. Ottinger. Sam could see how eager they were to please him.

"Give David a chance, Great-grandpa," Isabel

begged. She took hold of his firm hand and squeezed it hard. "Please?"

Mr. Ottinger gazed down at Isabel, and a faraway look came into his eyes. Sam wasn't sure, but she thought she saw his expression soften the slightest bit.

"All right," he said gruffly.

"Great! Oh, thank you, Great-grandpa," said Isabel.

Sam grinned at David and Joe. "Way to go, David!" she whispered. "Well, I'd better get to work."

She stopped at her first table and flipped open her pad. But as she began to take the order, she heard Isabel's great-grandfather speak up again.

"I'm warning you, Peter," he said. "If anything happens to Will's railway, you'll all be very sorry."

Chapter Four

Wishbone noticed that an uneasy silence fell over Pepper Pete's. Glancing up at his friends, the terrier saw that they were all watching Mr. Ottinger. As Mr. Ottinger said good-bye to Isabel, then walked toward the door with her parents, the stormy look never left his face.

"Wow!" Joe said, turning back to David and Isabel. "Was that remark meant as a threat?"

"I don't think Great-grandpa would really do anything," Isabel said slowly. "But it looks like he feels strongly about anything that reminds him of Will. If something happens to the model railway . . ."

"We'll all be very sorry," Sam finished, echoing Mr. Ottinger's last words. She had been at the next booth, but now she came over with her order pad to where her friends were seated. "It's almost like the curse in *The Moonstone*."

Wishbone glanced up at Sam with eager eyes. He knew Wilkie Collins's classic story well. "Talk about a great mystery. *The Moonstone* is one of my all-time favorites!"

"A curse?" Isabel said.

"There's a curse, all right. And it's a biggie!" Wishbone

barked, eager to tell the story. "You see, according to an ancient legend, disaster will come to anyone who—"

"Legend has it that disaster will happen to anyone who takes the Moonstone from its sacred shrine," Sam said. "And to anyone who keeps the diamond after that. So after Franklin Blake delivers the Moonstone to Rachel, he begins to worry all the more about what might happen to the diamond—and to Rachel."

"I guess we're worried, too," said David. "Except, I don't see what could happen to us that's so terrible, especially once I prevent the engine from going off the track."

Wishbone glanced up at David. "Obviously, you haven't been poked by Mr. Ottinger's cane yet!"

"I hope you're right," Sam said. "But I want to come along when you put in the rail, okay, David?"

"Me, too," said Isabel. "Great-grandpa might feel better if someone from our family is here."

"We might as well make it a party," Joe said. "Count me in."

"Sounds good," David agreed.

Sam glanced around Pepper Pete's. "I've still got more orders to take," she said, tapping her pad. "What do you want to eat?"

"Now we're talking!" Wishbone's tongue wagged. "How about a double pepperoni? Or cheese with meatballs and—"

"Let's have the special," Isabel said. "Mushrooms, pepperoni, and onions."

Wishbone barked his approval. "Good idea. It'll take at least three toppings to make me feel better after being poked by a cane and nearly run down by a train. . . . Oh—hi, Wanda. Hi, Ellen. You want pizza, too?"

Wishbone looked up to see Wanda and Ellen stop next to the booth. "Take a look at this," Wanda said. She pulled a rolled-up piece of poster paper from a large, bright green woven bag that was slung over her shoulder and opened it. "It's the poster for the costume party. This is part of the Oakdale History Month celebration."

Looking at the poster, Wishbone saw a drawing of a man and a woman. They wore old-fashioned turn-of-the-century outfits as they danced. At the top of the poster, bold letters read: DANCE THE NIGHT AWAY!

"This looks like fun," Sam said.

"It's going to be a wonderful party," Wanda told them. "We've booked the Greenville Players to do the music. And we have a volunteer to oversee the barbecue pit . . ."

"Barbecue?" Just hearing the word made Wishbone's mouth water. "Count me in, Wanda! I'll be the one dressed as a cute little dog."

"And, of course, the members of the Oakdale Historical Society and I have been working on the games—including an Oakdale History Quiz. The questions will be printed in Wednesday's *Chronicle,* and the winner will be announced Saturday at the gala. I've got the answer key right here." Wanda gave a mischievous smile as she pulled a folded sheet of paper from her bag. "There'll be great prizes. Trust me, this is one party you shouldn't miss."

"We won't," Joe promised.

Wishbone had seen Wanda in action often enough to know she put 110 percent of her enthusiasm and energy into all that she did. If she was organizing the party, it was bound to be fun.

"Of course, there is one drawback," Ellen said, frowning. "We were hoping to be able to hold the dance in a historical building, but the only place big enough for us to hold a town-wide event is in the school gym—not exactly a historical site."

DANCE THE NIGHT
AWAY!
SPECIAL

"We'll just have to make do, I suppose," Wanda said.

"Maybe not." Isabel straightened up, her dark eyes shining. "Our house is big, and old. There's a fountain, a covered entranceway, and gardens that have been there since the beginning of the century. We could have the party there!"

Wishbone's ears perked up. "Hundred-year-old gardens? Wow! When can I start digging?"

Wanda exchanged a look with Ellen, then said, "It sounds perfect. Do you think your family would agree to host the party? This is a big responsibility."

"I know Mom and Dad would love to. They like being involved with the town as much as I do," Isabel answered. With a slight frown, she added, "I'm not sure about Great-grandpa, but . . . Well, it can't hurt to ask. I'll talk to him and my parents, and then I'll let you know."

"Great!" Wanda said with an excited nod. "We'd have to make a last-minute change to the posters, but it would be worth it. Let me know as soon as you can."

Wanda rummaged in her bag for a slip of paper, wrote her phone number on it, and handed it to Isabel.

"See you at home, Joe. 'Bye, kids. 'Bye, Wishbone," Ellen said. Then, with a wave, she and Wanda were gone.

"'Bye!" Wishbone followed the two women with his eyes, then sniffed the air. "Pizza alert!"

Sam's father walked past to the next booth with a pizza on a metal tray. As he placed the slices onto individual plates, a cheesy tidbit dropped to the floor.

"I'll take care of that!" Wishbone trotted over, gobbled up the cheese, and then looked eagerly around. "Anyone else need my assistance?"

On his way back to Joe's booth, Wishbone felt something stiff and crinkly beneath his left front paw. Lifting his paw, he sniffed curiously.

"Joe, look!" Wishbone picked up a folded piece of paper in his teeth and carried it to Joe.

"What do you have there, boy?" Joe took the paper from Wishbone, unfolded it, and laid it in the center of the table. They leaned forward to see what it was. "Hey! It's the answer key to Miss Gilmore's Oakdale History Quiz. It must have fallen from her bag when she gave Isabel her phone number."

As Sam was reaching to take the paper, someone called out, "Hey, Sam! Are you ever going to stop goofing off and take our order?"

Looking over to where the voice had come from, Wishbone saw it was Joe's classmate Curtis. He and Damont were sitting with two other boys at the next booth. "That's no way to talk to my friend!" Wishbone said.

The boys didn't seem to hear. As they waited impatiently for Sam to come over, they looked back and forth from Sam's face to the paper Joe held.

Sam rolled her eyes. "I'll be right there," she told Curtis. "Joe, I'm going over to see Miss Gilmore about an ad for Pepper Pete's. Since I'm going over to the *Chronicle,* I can take the answer key to her. Now that we've seen the answers, she'll want to create a new puzzle."

Joe said, "Sure."

Taking the paper from Joe, she then walked over and tucked it behind the counter, next to the register. After doing that, Sam told her friends, "Now, I really need to go back to work." Then she went over to Curtis and Damont's booth.

"Looks like everything's under control." Wishbone glanced eagerly around the restaurant. Seeing a chunk of meatball under one of the booths, he pounced on it.

"Hi, guys!" Sam called to David and Joe early the next morning. It was Tuesday, and the boys were waiting for her outside Pepper Pete's. David was holding a small, bulging paper bag. "Is that what I think it is?" she asked hopefully.

David smiled and held up the bag. "One guardrail, ready for installation," he said. "I brought some special glue and paint, too."

Using the key her father had lent her, Sam unlocked the door and opened it. Joe hesitated, looking up and down the sidewalk. "Isabel's not here yet. Shouldn't we wait?"

"Not if we want to get to school on time," said Sam. "I'll leave the door open, but we'd better start without her."

As they went inside, Sam glanced around. She found the light switch that lit the back of the restaurant and turned it on. Every time she took a step, the sound echoed through the restaurant. Tables, chairs, and columns threw long, eerie shadows across the floor.

"It's kind of spooky, coming here when it's so quiet," she said. "I'm glad I'm not alone."

"Me, too," David said, looking around uneasily. "This won't take long." He headed for the model railway at the back of the restaurant, taking a customized small guardrail from his paper bag. "I'm going to need a drill and a screwdriver. I saw a toolbox yesterday. Do you know where it is, Sam?"

"Check under the platform. I saw it there yesterday," Joe said.

The bulky metal toolbox was a black rectangle among the shadows. Sam pulled it out and opened the heavy lid. Then she and Joe watched while David went to work. Within minutes, he had the guardrail securely screwed in and glued down next to the spot where the model engine had derailed.

"That ought to keep the train from running off the track," he said. "Now all we have to do is make sure it really works."

Sam crossed her fingers as David flipped the switch to start the train. As it chugged around the track, moving toward the tunnel, she felt a sense of anticipation build.

"Hold it!" Joe put up a hand and looked toward the entrance. "Did you guys hear that?"

Sam jumped uneasily. She hadn't heard anything except the train—at least, she didn't think so. But as she looked around, the hairs stood up on the back of her neck.

"Isabel?" Joe called out as he walked over to the entrance area.

Sam flipped the switch to stop the train. If Isabel was there, she would want to see the train in action. "Is she there?" Sam called over to Joe.

Joe looked around, then shook his head. "I guess I just imagined that I heard something."

As Sam looked around, the funny sensation at the back of her neck remained. She couldn't rid herself of the feeling that someone was watching them.

Get a grip! she thought. Shaking herself, Sam turned back to the model railway and flipped the switch on again. This time, there were no interruptions—and no disasters. When the train reached the downhill curve after coming out of the tunnel, it chugged around it without any problem.

"You did it, David!" said Joe, giving the thumb's-up sign.

Sam let out a sigh of relief. "Great! I want to get a few photos for the special edition of the school paper," she said, reaching for her backpack. "Then we can head to school."

Sam worked as quickly as she could. While she snapped a few shots, Joe took the paint David had brought and painted the new guardrail.

"Nice," said Sam. "That brown matches the wood of the model fences almost exactly. I bet even Mr. Ottinger won't be able to find anything wrong with the repair."

She tried to sound optimistic, but she couldn't shake the uneasy feeling that had come over her. She was glad when they were finally done with their work. After leaving a note for her dad, they locked up and left.

"I wonder why Isabel didn't show up," Joe said as they stood outside. "She said she'd be here."

Sam looked up and down the sidewalk, but there was no sign of Isabel. "Something must have come up," she said, setting her backpack over one shoulder. "I guess I'll find out what when I see her in first period."

But when Sam reached homeroom, Isabel wasn't there. Sam didn't see Isabel all day, including at the newspaper meeting after school.

"She must be out sick," Sam told Joe and David when they met her at her locker after school. "I talked to the editor of the paper. She's already interviewing Ethan Johnstone for the History Month special edition, but she would like to include Isabel's interview with her great-grandfather, too."

Ethan Johnstone was a name with which Sam, Joe, and David were all familiar. His great-great-grandfather, Moses Johnstone, had founded the town of Oakdale some one hundred fifty years earlier.

"Ethan Johnstone must be pretty old himself. It

would be great to compare what he has to say with what Mr. Ottinger remembers," said Joe.

"If Mr. Ottinger agrees to do the interview," Sam said. "Isabel wasn't at all sure he would."

"Let's try calling her when we get to Pepper Pete's," David suggested. "I want to stop by there to see how the repair to the railway is holding up."

Sam was relieved to hear she wasn't the only one who was still thinking about the model railway. She was sure everything was fine. But something in her wanted to make absolutely sure.

Twenty minutes later, Sam, David, and Joe walked into Pepper Pete's. This time there were no shadows, no creepy echoes. There were just the employees and a few customers, talking and eating.

"Hi, Wishbone." Joe grinned as his dog trotted over with his tail wagging. "I should have known you'd be here."

"Sometimes I think Wishbone is our best customer," Sam added. "He's always ready . . ."

Her voice trailed off when she saw a uniformed police officer standing at the counter. She recognized the stocky man as Officer Krulla, from the Oakdale Police Department. He was talking to her father—and they both looked very serious.

"Dad?" Sam asked, hurrying over. "What is going on?"

Her father turned to her with a worried expression on his face. "Sam! Thank goodness you're here. Did you notice anything unusual this morning when you were in here?"

Sam swallowed hard. Was it possible she'd overlooked something? But as she thought back, she was sure she hadn't. "No. David made the repairs on the railway and we left shortly after," she answered.

"We were with her," Joe said, as he and David came over. "Why? Did something happen?"

"Yes." Sam's father frowned as he motioned toward the platform at the back of the restaurant. "It's the model railway. When I got here to open up before lunch—"

"The engine!" Sam cried, following her dad's gaze. "It's gone!"

Chapter Five

"The engine's . . . *gone?*" Wishbone's tail went stiff. He trotted to the back of the restaurant with Sam, David, and Joe. Rising up on his hind legs and leaning against the platform, Wishbone skimmed over the panorama with his alert canine eyes. Sure enough, the gleaming black engine was nowhere to be seen. Half a dozen passenger and freight cars still sat on the rails.

"I'm sure the engine was here when we left this morning," Sam said. She turned worried eyes toward her father, who stepped from behind the counter and walked to the model railway with Officer Krulla. "Are you sure it's missing? I mean, do you think it was *stolen?*"

Sam's father nodded. "I didn't notice anything unusual when I first got here. The place was locked up, same as always. I accidentally dropped some olive oil on the floor behind the counter, so I was busy cleaning it up for a while. Then there were some deliveries." He nodded toward some boxes that were piled up next to the double doors that led to the kitchen and bathrooms. "I'd already been here for more than an hour before I happened to look back here," he explained. "That was when I realized the engine wasn't there, and I called the police."

"Whoa! Looks like we've got a mystery on our paws." Wishbone jumped back down onto all fours and gazed up at Officer Krulla, his tail wagging. "Luckily, I'm just the dog to get to the bottom of it. So, if you would bring me up to speed . . ."

"I conducted a brief search," Officer Krulla told Sam, David, and Joe.

"No engine?" David guessed.

"Afraid not," the officer answered, shaking his head. "What's curious is that I didn't see any signs of a break-in, either. The lunch rush made it hard for me to do my work, though, and Mr. Kepler was busy. I decided to come back now, while there were fewer people."

Wishbone's ears perked up as Pepper Pete's front door banged open. He turned to see Isabel race into the restaurant.

"Hi, everyone!" she called, as she walked to the back of the restaurant. Her cheeks were flushed, and her brown eyes sparkled.

"Hi, Isabel," Joe greeted her. "Where were you today? We didn't see you in school."

"I was . . . uh . . . out sick," Isabel said in a rush. Her eyes searched out the model railway behind Sam, Joe, David, and Wishbone. "But I feel a lot better now, so I came to see how David's repair—"

She broke off talking and frowned at the railway.

"What happened to the engine?" she asked with alarm.

Wishbone saw the uncomfortable glances that ricocheted among Sam, Joe, David, and Sam's father. They looked as unhappy as Wishbone was when he got his yearly shots. No one was looking forward to breaking the news of the missing engine to Isabel.

"I'm afraid I've got some bad news," Mr. Kepler said. He stepped over to Isabel and began to tell her what had happened. As Isabel listened, the color drained from her cheeks.

"The engine was *stolen?*" she said, when Sam's father was finished. "But that ruins everything!"

"I'm so sorry," Sam said. "Dad already reported the theft to the police."

"You can be certain I'll do everything in my power to track down the stolen engine," Officer Krulla assured everyone.

"So will we," said Joe.

Wishbone barked his promise along with Joe's. "Joe and I make a great team. And when it comes to tracking, no one has more experience than I do!"

Despite all their promises, Isabel didn't look any happier. "Great-grandpa is going to hit the roof when he finds out," she said.

Sam and her father both looked concerned. "I can't tell you how sorry I am," Mr. Kepler said. "Naturally, I accept full responsibility, since the model engine was taken from my restaurant."

"You didn't do anything wrong," David spoke up.

"Somehow, I don't think Mr. Ottinger will be as generous as you are," Sam told David. "He said we'd all be sorry if anything happened to the train, and now it's gone. I know he's going to blame us."

Wishbone didn't like to see Sam and her dad looking so glum. "Cheer up, Sam." He trotted over and licked her hand, but Sam didn't smile.

"There's got to be something we can do," Joe said.

"I'm not sure what," Sam said with a shrug. She

slipped her hands into her jacket pockets—and then blinked. "Unless . . ."

She pulled *The Moonstone* from one of her pockets, a fresh look of determination in her eyes. "Maybe there *is* something we can do," she said. "After all, Franklin Blake didn't give up after the Moonstone was taken."

"So, someone stole the diamond a second time?" David asked.

Sam nodded. "It was taken from Rachel's dressing room the night of her birthday," she explained. "Franklin Blake felt responsible because he had delivered it to her. So he called in a detective, Sergeant Cuff. He discovered clues by going over the scene of the crime—and studying everything that happened before the theft—in the greatest detail." She tapped the book, then smiled at her friends. "It seems to me that we could do the same thing here."

"Great idea, Sam!" Wishbone barked his approval. His alert eyes searched out Officer Krulla. He had taken Sam's father aside and was talking to him at the counter. "Hey, guys! Mind if we get a head start on the investigation?"

"I've heard it's important not to disturb a crime scene," Isabel said.

"Me, too," said Sam. "But we can't just stand by and do nothing. . . ."

She went over to her father and Officer Krulla, then came back smiling a moment later. "They said it's okay to look," she reported, "as long as we don't disturb or move anything."

Wishbone put his nose to the floor and started to sniff the area near the model railway. He had gone only a few feet when he heard Sam draw in her breath sharply.

"I found something!" she said.

In a flash, Isabel, Joe, David, Walter, and Officer Krulla had surrounded Sam. As they bent over the model railway, Wishbone rose up on his hind legs so he could see, too.

"Look at the paint on the railing," Sam said. She pointed to the guardrail David had installed that morning. "It's been smudged!"

Looking closely, Wishbone saw a spot on the guardrail where the brown paint had rubbed off.

"I was really careful when I painted the guardrail," Joe said. "I know it was completely covered when we left."

"There definitely wasn't a smudge," Sam agreed. "I would have noticed it when I took photos after the repair. And since we didn't touch it, someone else must have come in while the paint was still wet. Wow!" she said, shaking her head in amazement. "It's just like what happened in *The Moonstone!*"

"How?" Isabel asked. "What's so important about a smudge?"

Wishbone gave an excited bark. "That's exactly what

Sergeant Cuff had to figure out in the book. Tell her, Sam!"

"Sergeant Cuff found a smudge on the door to Rachel's dressing room," Sam explained. "The door had just been varnished. By estimating when the varnish had dried, Sergeant Cuff was able to determine at about what time the thief had struck."

"The paint I brought was quick-drying," David said. "It would have dried within an hour."

"So . . ."—Isabel stared seriously at the smudged rail—". . . whoever took the model engine must have broken in right after you guys left."

Wishbone glanced up at his friends, his tail wagging excitedly. "Now, if we could just find out who it was, and how the person got in—"

"I just thought of something!" Joe said suddenly. "I think the person might have come into Pepper Pete's *before* we left."

"Come again?" Wishbone looked up curiously at his best buddy.

"But we would have seen anyone who came in," David said.

"Not necessarily," Joe said. "I think I heard the person. Remember I thought Isabel was at the door?"

This was all news to Wishbone. He sat back and listened while Joe, Sam, and David talked it over.

"Me?" Isabel looked at Joe in surprise. "But I wasn't anywhere near here. I was . . . home sick, remember?" she said.

Wishbone saw her glance nervously at her feet while she spoke. But Joe and the others were so busy talking that they didn't notice her reaction.

"Then who could it have been?" David asked.

"I don't know," Sam said, shrugging. "All I know is

that we were paying attention to the model railway, not the front-entrance door. And the railway is at the rear of the restaurant. Someone could have come in without us noticing."

"That would explain why we didn't find evidence that the lock had been tampered with," said Officer Krulla. "The thief could have hidden somewhere until after you left."

Wishbone wagged his tail, proud of his best buddy's fine detective work. "Sounds like a good theory to me. 'Atta boy, Joe!"

Sam's father pointed toward the double doors in the side wall next to the counter. "The kitchen, restrooms, and storage closet would be good hiding spots. They are back there," he said.

"I'm on the case, guys!" Wishbone trotted toward the doorway—then stopped when he picked up the smell of one of his favorite snacks. "Mmm-mmm! A potato chip. Be with you as soon as I eat this. . . ."

He made quick work of the chip, then scooted forward when he saw another one . . . and another. The potato chips led Wishbone through the double doors and into the back hallway. There were still half a dozen chips in sight, when Joe tugged on Wishbone's collar.

"No, Wishbone. We're not supposed to touch anything until after the police have finished going over the restaurant, including checking out the chips," Joe said sternly.

Wishbone watched longingly as Officer Krulla and Sam's dad followed the trail of chips to a closed door at the end of the hall.

"That's the storage closet," Mr. Kepler said. He opened the door and turned on the light, then frowned. "Someone's been in here."

Wishbone trotted the rest of the way to the closet. Rows of shelves—filled with aprons, napkins, cutlery, plates, and unopened cardboard boxes of supplies—lined the walls. Wishbone saw a crumpled potato-chip bag on the floor in front of the shelves. Several mouth-watering crumbs lay scattered around it. "Aha!"

"So someone was hiding," Isabel said, as she, Joe, Sam, and David came over to the closet.

"Once we were gone, whoever it was took the model engine," Joe added. "When he or she grabbed it, the thief probably smudged the fresh paint of the guardrail."

"Makes sense," said Officer Krulla. "You kids would have had to leave at what time—eight-thirty or so?"

David nodded.

"And Mr. Kepler said he arrived to open up at about . . ."—Officer Krulla glanced quickly at his notepad—". . . nine o'clock. You probably took the thief by surprise when you showed up, Mr. Kepler."

"I don't usually start setting up until ten. But today I was expecting deliveries, so I came earlier than usual," said Mr. Kepler. "The thief would have had to hide somewhere with the engine until he or she could get out. I guess whoever it was decided to have a snack."

Sam's father nodded, still gazing at the crumpled chips bag. "I had the radio on the whole time I was cleaning up that olive oil," he said. "Someone could have sneaked out without my knowing it."

"I'll need you all to clear out of the hallway so I can finish examining the area," said Officer Krulla.

That was fine with Wishbone. He preferred the main room of the restaurant. That was where the pizza and breadsticks were!

As he trotted back into the dining area, the terrier gazed longingly at the counter. "Pizza's not part of the crime scene, is it, Joe?" the terrier said, gazing up at his best friend.

But Joe didn't answer. He had crouched down and was looking at something on the floor in front of the counter.

Going over to Joe, Wishbone spotted a folded sheet of paper that looked very familiar. "Isn't that the answer key to Wanda's Oakdale History Quiz?"

"You guys, look at this," Joe said to David, Sam, and Isabel as he picked up the paper. "It's the answer key to Miss Gilmore's Oakdale History Quiz."

Wishbone sighed. "No one ever listens to the dog."

"What's it doing here?" Sam asked. She came over next to Joe and frowned. "I put it behind the counter yesterday to take to Miss Gilmore. I forgot. But I did call her. Dad, did you move it?"

Mr. Kepler shook his head as he came through the double doors from the hallway. "No, I did not. The only papers I've touched today are paper napkins and sheets from the order pad," he said. He shot a curious look at Sam. "Why? Do you think the thief looked at the answers while he or she was here?"

Joe shrugged and said, "I can't think of anyone else who could have moved it."

"I guess anything's possible. We'll have to wait and see what the police come up with," Sam's father said. "In the meantime, there's something I've got to do."

"What's that?" Sam asked.

"I have to tell Mr. Ottinger that the engine from his model railway has been stolen," said Mr. Kepler. "And, believe me, I'm not looking forward to it."

Wishbone gazed through the car window as Sam's father turned into Isabel's driveway fifteen minutes later.

Up ahead, a large stone house sprawled across an enormous, grassy lawn. Bushy azaleas ran along the edges of the house, and two big oak trees towered overhead. The sight of the lawn made Wishbone want to leap from the car and start exploring. "Where are your dogs, Isabel? I can't wait to meet them!"

Joe and Isabel sat beside him in the backseat, while Sam sat up front with her dad. Wishbone was glad he and Joe had decided to tag along. Besides getting to meet Iggy and Axel, Wishbone wanted to be there when Sam and her father broke the bad news to Isabel's family. David would have come, too, but he had to go home to baby-sit his little sister, Emily.

"Well, here goes," said Mr. Kepler. He stopped the car beneath a covered archway in front of the entrance. Then he took a deep breath and reached for the door.

Joe opened the back door of the car, and Wishbone jumped to the ground and headed for the front door.

"You'd better wait out in the front yard, Wishbone," Isabel said. "Great-grandpa is still getting used to Iggy and Axel. I don't think he'd be too happy to find you sniffing around his antiques, too."

"We won't be long, boy," Joe said, scratching Wishbone behind the ears.

As Wishbone watched his friends disappear behind the front door, he felt disappointed. But with the smells of budding plants and freshly cut grass calling out to him, Wishbone couldn't feel bad for long. Even if he couldn't stay with Sam and her father to give them moral support, he might be able to find Isabel's dogs.

Soon, the Jack Russell terrier was trotting happily from place to place, sniffing and digging. "Yes!" Wishbone barked, eagerly smelling the roots of one of the old oaks. "Iggy and Axel have left their mark, but . . . where are they?"

He trotted around one side of the stone house, still sniffing for dogs. There was a wide terrace at the back of the house, but Wishbone didn't see any dogs playing there. Stone stairs led from the terrace to the largest gardens Wishbone had ever seen.

At the center of one of the gardens was a large stone fountain. Statues of three dolphins appeared to leap from the water. Gravel paths led away from the fountain in every direction, disappearing among trees, hedges, and more flowerbeds than Wishbone could count.

"Wow! This isn't just a backyard—it's an amusement park for dogs! Iggy and Axel *must* be in here somewhere. . . ." Tail wagging, Wishbone took off down the nearest path. Up ahead, rosebushes climbed a series of trellises, open wooden arches that curved over the path.

Just like the garden in The Moonstone, thought Wishbone.

Wishbone recalled that Sergeant Cuff was an excellent rose gardener who spent hours walking among the Verinders' roses as he tried to figure out who had stolen the Moonstone. Of course, Wishbone felt the story would have been even better if there had been some dogs to enjoy the garden, too.

Suddenly, Wishbone stopped and sniffed the air. He picked up the same canine scents he'd smelled on the oak tree! Iggy and Axel were somewhere nearby. . . .

Hearing a rustling noise beyond the roses, Wishbone ran toward it, barking joyfully. Just beyond the last trellis, he saw two black-and-brown German shepherds. They were arguing over a rubber bone, trying to pull it from each other.

"Boy, am I glad to finally meet you two!" Wishbone trotted closer to the German shepherds, his tail wagging. "You must be Iggy and Axel. I'm—"

Grrrrrr!

The German shepherds dropped the rubber bone and bared their teeth at him. Wishbone stopped short, staring at them in surprise. "That's not quite the greeting I was expecting, guys."

Grrrrrr!

"Wow! Isabel wasn't kidding when she said you two needed to be trained." Wishbone puffed out his chest and walked a few steps closer to Iggy and Axel. "Luckily, I happen to be a very charming and well-mannered dog. I can show you—"

Before Wishbone could finish, both German shepherds lunged at him. Wishbone yelped and scooted backward—just in time. The dogs' teeth clamped down on the air right next to his tail.

"Hey! I happen to be very attached to my tail—and I'd like to keep it that way!" Wishbone quickly sized up

the situation. He'd hoped to make new friends. But it was obvious that Iggy and Axel weren't in the mood to meet an older, wiser canine. The two German shepherds came at him again, barking and growling.

"Yikes!" Wishbone sent dirt flying as he ran away—with Iggy and Axel right behind him in hot pursuit. "Time for a strategic withdrawal. In other words . . . I am outta here!"

Chapter Six

Sam sat on the edge of an overstuffed couch she shared with Joe and Isabel in Mr. Ottinger's living room. The room was filled with antique furniture, paintings, and rugs. Two bay windows and a pair of large glass-paned doors overlooked a terrace and the gardens. Sam could practically feel the history of the place.

And the mystery. There she was, sitting in the very house where the golden dog had disappeared. But she was too worried about why they were there to take in much of the scenery.

Sam had known it was going to be difficult to tell Mr. Ottinger about the missing engine. But she hadn't known it would be this hard. As Sam had anticipated, Mr. Ottinger had taken the news badly. As soon as he'd learned the model engine was stolen, he became very angry.

"I *knew* putting Will's railway on display was a mistake," Mr. Ottinger said. "Mr. Kepler, the lack of security in your restaurant is criminal!"

"The police are doing everything possible to get the engine back," said Sam's father. He looked so miserable, Sam's heart went out to him.

"I've half a mind to press charges against you," the old man said to Mr. Kepler, as if he hadn't even heard what her father had said.

"Dad didn't do anything wrong!" Sam spoke up.

"Young lady . . ." Mr. Ottinger turned his piercing gaze at her. Sam braced herself. Even if Mr. Ottinger was one of the most powerful men in Oakdale, she couldn't remain silent while he treated her father unfairly.

But to her surprise, Mr. Ottinger's face suddenly softened. For a long moment, he simply looked back and forth from her, to Joe, to Isabel. "You young folks," he said gruffly. "You're just like Wi——"

He stopped in mid-sentence and seemed to shake himself. "Will's toy engine is gone," he said. He was all business again, his bushy white eyebrows bunched in a straight line across his forehead. "And someone is going to pay the price."

Mr. Ottinger glared at Sam's father. "I want what is left of the model railway brought here immediately," Mr. Ottinger demanded.

"Please don't do anything yet, Great-grandpa," Isabel said. "I'm sure the police will get back the engine, if you just give them a little time."

Mr. Ottinger turned toward Isabel, and again Sam saw the hard edge leave his face. "I'll wait until Saturday," he agreed. "If the engine isn't back by then, I want the rest of the railway returned. Mr. Kepler, the engine was stolen due to your lack of security. The community has a right to know their belongings aren't safe in your establishment. I will make this public if the engine is not located."

Sam felt her spirits sink. It was already Tuesday. That gave them just four days to find the engine. . . .

Loud sounds of barking and growling interrupted

Sam's thoughts. The noise had come from somewhere outside in the gardens. It was so loud that everyone in the room turned to look.

"What is that awful noise?" Mr. Ottinger complained.

"Sounds like Iggy and Axel," Isabel said.

"And Wishbone," Joe added, grimacing.

Sam felt a sense of uneasiness about the sound of the barking. It was so . . . fierce. "Something's wrong!" she said, jumping to her feet.

Isabel hurried to the doors, and Sam and Joe followed. Throwing the doors open wide, Isabel ran onto the terrace. Sam followed her to the railing and scanned the gardens. "I don't see them, but—"

Just then a fresh round of barking broke out. Sam, Isabel, and Joe followed it. They ran down the terrace steps, past a fountain, and down a gravel path toward trellises covered with rose vines. The path was littered with dirt and broken-up flowers. Sam saw that the path ended beyond the trellises, in a grassy circle surrounded by thick hedges.

"There!" she called out.

Wishbone had been cornered in front of the hedges by two German shepherds. All three dogs were growling, barking, and baring their teeth.

"Iggy, Axel . . . stop!" Isabel ordered. She grabbed her dogs by their collars and pulled them back toward the roses.

"Wishbone! Are you all right?" Joe bent down next to his dog and began petting him.

"He doesn't seem to be hurt," Sam said, crouching down next to Wishbone. "That's what's—"

"Look at this mess." Mr. Ottinger's stern voice spoke up behind them.

Sam turned around to see Isabel's great-grandfather

standing beneath the arch of rose vines. He poked his cane at a wooden slat that had broken off one of the trellises, then kicked at some uprooted flowers. "The garden is a shambles!"

"I'm sorry, Mr. Ottinger," Joe said. "I'll help pay for the damage."

"Sorry, Great-grandpa," said Isabel. "I don't know why I'm having such a hard time training them. I guess that obedience class I took them to didn't help much."

Wishbone let out a bark that seemed to say he agreed.

Sam sighed as she looked at the uprooted flowers—and the frown on Mr. Ottinger's face.

If things continue like this, she thought, *Oakdale History Month is going to be a disaster.*

Wishbone was glad when he, Joe, Sam, and Mr. Kepler returned to Pepper Pete's. While Sam went to get an apron and an order pad, her dad went to work behind the counter.

Wishbone followed Joe to one of the booths, and before long he sniffed the mouth-watering smells of cheese and meatballs. Looking around, he noticed Pepper Pete's was as busy as ever. Seeing Mr. Kepler serve a pizza, he trotted on over to the table. He was so busy sniffing he didn't see who was sitting there—until one of the occupants spoke to him.

"What are you doing here, Wishbone?"

Wishbone looked up to see Damont Jones. He was with Curtis and two other boys Wishbone recognized from Joe's school. Most kids from Sequoyah Middle School usually liked to play with Wishbone or, even better, give him treats. But Damont just stared at him.

"Hi, guys." Wishbone smiled at the boys, his tail wagging. "I'm conducting a survey on customer satisfaction

here at Pepper Pete's. On a scale of one to ten, how would you rate that pizza?"

It was obvious to Wishbone that the pizza was top-notch. But he couldn't tell whether Damont agreed. Instead of answering, Damont called out to Joe, "Hey, Talbot! Can't you stop your dog from bothering the customers?"

"I'll have you know I'm here on important business," Wishbone said, letting out a bark. "But if you won't participate in my survey . . ."

Wishbone noticed a bit of cheese laced with meat-ball that dangled from the edge of the tray. It looked as if it were about to drop to the floor. Edging his muzzle closer to the tray, Wishbone managed to catch the tidbit in midair. "Definitely a ten—or even a twelve."

"Come on, Wishbone!" Joe called out from his booth. He started toward Wishbone, but Sam beat him to it. She finished taking an order at the next booth, then turned to Wishbone with a frown.

"Wishbone," Sam said, "you have to behave—"

She stopped in mid-sentence. Wishbone gazed curiously at her. "But I am behaving!"

Sam didn't reply. She was staring at Damont. Her eyes were glued to the sleeve of his yellow-corduroy shirt.

"What's the matter?" Wishbone turned his alert eyes back to Damont—then he wagged his tail furiously. "Hey! Isn't that paint on your cuff? *Brown* paint?"

Without waiting for an answer, Wishbone trotted to the back of the restaurant. He rose up on his hind legs and looked at the guardrail David had installed that morning. "Yup! It's the same color, all right. But . . . how did that paint get on Damont's shirt?"

Wishbone hurried back to Damont's booth and gazed up at Sam. "Are you wondering the same thing I am? Could *Damont* have stolen the model engine?"

Chapter Seven

Sam couldn't stop staring at the brown paint on Damont's sleeve. Was it possible that Damont was the person who had sneaked into Pepper Pete's? Had he stolen the model engine?

Sam frowned, trying to think through the situation. She didn't want to think Damont would do anything so illegal. Sure, he had made some trouble in the past. But stealing a valuable antique? Sam just couldn't imagine him committing such a crime.

"Uh . . . Sam?" Damont said, breaking into her thoughts. "Are you going to do something about Wishbone?"

Sam blinked. "Oh—sorry. Come on, Wishbone." Taking hold of Wishbone's collar, she led him over to Joe's booth. "Joe, you're not going to believe this . . ."

In a low voice, Sam told him about the brown paint on Damont's sleeve.

"He must be the person who stole the model engine," Sam concluded.

"But how are we going to prove it?" Joe asked. "Damont's not going to admit it."

"No . . ." Sam stared across Pepper Pete's at Damont, then snapped her fingers. "But he might admit something else. Think about it. My dad didn't open up until nine. If Damont was already inside, he couldn't have gotten to class until after that."

"Which means he would have been late to school," Joe said, giving an excited nod. "If we can *prove* he was late, that makes him even more of a suspect."

Sam nodded. "You and Wishbone wait here," she told Joe. "I'm going to see what I can find out."

When Sam got to Damont's booth, she smiled and said, "Sorry about Wishbone. How's the pizza?"

Damont gave the thumb's-up sign. "Good," he said. The other boys nodded their agreement.

Trying to sound casual, Sam asked, "Did any of you guys take the social-studies test today? It was a killer."

Sam knew there were two eighth-grade social studies classes on Tuesdays; one first thing in the morning, and one in the afternoon. Damont wasn't in the afternoon class with her, so she figured he had to be in the morning class.

"It was tough," agreed one of Damont's friends, a boy with sandy hair and freckles. He elbowed Damont in the ribs and added, "Not that Damont would know. He didn't even get to school until after the test was over."

Yes! thought Sam. *So Damont* was *late to school this morning*. Aloud, she just said, "Oh, yeah? Where were you, Damont?"

Damont didn't answer. Sam noticed that he wouldn't look her in the eye, either.

"That's a nice shirt," she said. "Too bad there's paint on it."

Sam pointed toward his sleeve, and Damont did a double-take. Sam had a feeling he hadn't even known that the brown paint was there until that second. Seeing the uneasy way he stared down at it made her even more suspicious.

Shooting a probing glance at Damont, Sam said, "It looks like you've been around some wet paint."

"I was . . . uh . . . painting my bike. . . . Not that it's any of your business," Damont said. With that, he got to his feet and headed for the bathroom.

All Sam's instincts told her Damont was lying. And he'd seemed very eager to get away from her questions—as if he had something to hide.

Just like in The Moonstone, Sam thought, as she watched Damont disappear into the back hallway.

There had been lots of guests and servants at the Verinders' home when the diamond was stolen. Some of them came and went mysteriously, without explaining themselves. Others lied or refused to answer when Sergeant Cuff and Franklin Blake questioned them. Even Rachel herself wouldn't cooperate. The characters had many secrets, and that added to the story's sense of mystery. It also made Sergeant Cuff's job more difficult.

He certainly has his work cut out for him, thought Sam. *And so do I.*

"So, you think Damont is the person who took the model engine?" Isabel asked Sam Wednesday morning at school.

Sam had found Isabel at her locker before their first class. She filled Isabel in on what had happened at Pepper Pete's the day before. "The paint on Damont's shirt was the exact same brown as we used on the rail," Sam said. "When I asked Damont about it, he acted really weird."

"I bet he took it!" Isabel said, her eyes gleaming with intensity. "I've got to prove it and get Will's engine back for Great-grandpa."

"The question is: *How* do we prove it?" Sam said. "I think we should start by talking to him—where he can't avoid us by walking away. Even if he doesn't admit he took the engine, he might make some kind of slip."

"Sounds like a good plan," said Isabel, as she closed her locker.

The two girls were on their way to their first class when they saw Joe and David in the hall. David was holding a copy of *The Oakdale Chronicle*, and he and Joe were looking at it. When they saw Sam and Isabel, David quickly lowered the newspaper.

"Uh . . . hi, Sam. Hi, Isabel," Joe said, shooting an uncomfortable glance at David.

"Hi, guys," Sam said. "Is something wrong?"

David hesitated, then said, "You're not going to like this, but . . . I guess you should see it."

He held out the newspaper, pointing to an article on the front page. Sam's breath caught in her throat when she saw the headline:

ANTIQUE RAILWAY ENGINE MISSING

"Does it mention Pepper Pete's?" she asked.

Joe nodded. "It's all in the first few paragraphs," he said.

Sam skimmed over the story of how her father had arrived at Pepper Pete's to find the model engine missing. It seemed straightforward—until she got to the third paragraph. The article read:

> In an interview, Mr. Carl Ottinger, an esteemed citizen of Oakdale and the owner of the model railway, expressed his family's "deep concern" about the missing model engine. "I had second thoughts about putting the model railway on display at Pepper Pete's," Mr. Ottinger said. "Now a valuable antique is gone. . . ."

Sam couldn't bring herself to read any farther. "Oh, no," she moaned. "He makes it sound as if Pepper Pete's is responsible for the theft! We did everything right—we took all precautions. If people take this the wrong way, my dad could lose a lot of business."

"A reporter called the house last night. I wish Great-grandpa had never talked to him," Isabel said. She gave Sam a pleading look. "Please say you won't let it get in the way of our being friends."

"Of course I won't," Sam reassured her.

Isabel let out her breath, looking relieved. "Good. Because I was hoping you could come over to my house this afternoon. Great-grandpa said he'd let me interview him for the school paper and, well . . . I thought maybe you could come take photos."

Sam hesitated. After reading the article . . .

"Please?" Isabel asked. "Great-grandpa is starting to open up, but sometimes he just clams up. And I cannot figure out why."

Sam recalled how Mr. Ottinger reacted the day before when he mentioned Will's name. "How do you think I can help?" she asked.

"He seems nicer when other kids are around," Isabel answered. "I just figured if you were there, too . . ."

Sam could see how important the interview was to Isabel. And she had promised to take photos for the special edition.

"Okay," she agreed. "I'll do it."

Chapter Eight

Wishbone woke up from his afternoon nap on Wednesday to see Ellen and Wanda sitting on the living room couch. They were looking at a notebook Wanda held. Several other books lay open on the coffee table in front of them.

"We're almost done," Wanda said. "One more question and the new Oakdale History Quiz will be finished. Thanks for helping me, Ellen."

"Why didn't you ask me to help, Wanda?" Wishbone's ears perked up. He jumped down from the chair he was napping in and gazed at Ellen and Wanda. "This dog has many skills."

"I'm glad to help out, especially if it means making sure no one has an unfair advantage," said Ellen. "Joe told me he, Sam, David, and Isabel saw the answer key to the puzzle before they realized what it was. Plus, it looks like others may have seen the answer key or gotten the answers."

A cool spring breeze blew through the open window. It reminded Wishbone that he, too, should be getting busy. He ran to his doggie door and pushed through it.

Mr. Ottinger's Saturday deadline was just three days away. Wishbone was determined to help Sam sniff out the thief. But Damont was their number-one suspect, and he was still in school. That left Wishbone with some free time, and he knew just what to do.

"Time to look up some German shepherds in great need of guidance!" Wishbone trotted to the edge of the Talbots' yard, then hesitated.

Iggy and Axel hadn't been very good listeners the day before. He would need something special to help break the ice.

"I know!" Wishbone ran over to Wanda's yard. Just the week before, he had buried a prime soup bone among the flowerbeds there. With his keen nose, it was easy for him to find the spot and dig up the bone. Wishbone took the bone in his teeth and shook the excess dirt from it. "No dog could resist this!"

A while later, Wishbone reached the old stone house on the outskirts of Oakdale. He trotted up the curving drive, then circled around to the back of the house.

"Grrrrrr!"

The deep-throated sound was coming from the terrace. Glancing in the direction of the steps, Wishbone caught sight of Iggy and Axel. The two dogs were growling as they attacked a rubber bone, trying to rip it to pieces. They didn't appear to have smelled Wishbone. He headed for the steps, with the soup bone still in his mouth.

"Okay, let'sh shtart wif lesshon number one: Save the serioush attitude for serioush situations, like chasing cats."

Wishbone had taken only a few steps when the terrace doors opened, and a heavyset woman stepped outside. "Iggy, Axel . . . come inside!"

She grabbed the dogs' collars and pulled them inside, shutting the doors behind them. Wishbone sighed as he watched them go. "Now, what?"

He glanced over his haunches at the dolphin fountain and the gardens around it. "Hmm . . . I didn't get a chance to explore yesterday."

Wishbone quickly buried his bone in the soft earth at the foot of the terrace. Then he trotted toward the fountain with his tongue lolling.

"It looks like now's my chance!"

Sam's camera was tucked inside her backpack as she coasted her bike into the curved driveway that led to Isabel's house after school that afternoon. As she stared at the covered entrance, she imagined herself riding up to the Verinders' estate in the English countryside.

Sam had gotten to the best part of *The Moonstone* by then. The story had gone through a lot of plot twists and turns, and the characters were as secretive as ever. More and more, Sam had the feeling that their formal language and extreme politeness covered up something. But she still didn't know what the secrets were—or who had stolen the Moonstone.

Or who stole the model engine.

With a sigh, she parked her bike under the covered entrance, and rang the bell. A moment later Isabel opened the door.

"Hi!" Isabel greeted her. "Come on in. I was just helping Mrs. Hazlett make some iced tea."

Sam followed Isabel past an old grandfather clock and down a long hallway to a spacious, sunny kitchen at the back of the house. A large woman was standing at a counter, stirring a pitcher of iced tea. Isabel's two dogs were eating from metal bowls near the back door.

"This is my friend Sam," Isabel told the housekeeper. "Sam, meet Mrs. Hazlett."

"Nice to meet you," Sam said.

"Hello, there, Sam," Mrs. Hazlett said, with a warm smile. As she spoke, she poured iced tea into three glasses that were lined up on the counter. There was something both friendly and efficient about Mrs. Hazlett. Sam liked her right away. "Mr. Ottinger is waiting for you in the library," said the housekeeper.

Isabel grabbed a glass of iced tea in one hand and a notebook in the other. "Well, here goes," she said. Giving Sam a nervous smile, she started back down the hall. "I know Great-grandpa agreed to talk, but I can never tell when he's going to shut me out. There's so much I need to know! About the golden dog . . . about everything."

As Sam followed with the two other glasses, she could see how nervous Isabel was. She knew Isabel was hoping the interview would bring her and her great-grandfather closer together. Sam hoped it would, too.

Isabel led the way to a door near the foyer. When she opened it, Sam saw wall-to-wall bookcases and dark leather furniture. Mr. Ottinger was sitting in an armchair with a book in his lap. His thick white hair was brushed back from his forehead, and he was wearing glasses. His carved wooden cane leaned against the arm of his chair.

"Time for our interview, Great-grandpa," Isabel announced, with a hesitant smile.

Upon seeing Isabel, Mr. Ottinger took off his glasses and smiled. "Hello, Isabel." Then he greeted Sam.

So far, so good, thought Sam. He actually seemed happy to see them.

"Hi, Mr. Ottinger," she said, placing the two glasses

of iced tea on coasters on a coffee table. "I'm here to take photographs to go with the interview."

Isabel put the third glass of iced tea on the table next to her great-grandfather, then opened her notebook. "Are you ready?"

Mr. Ottinger closed his book and nodded. "I've been looking forward to talking with my favorite great-granddaughter," he said.

This was a side of Mr. Ottinger Sam hadn't seen before. He was being so nice, almost joking with Isabel—nothing like the stern elderly man Sam had seen and heard.

"I'm your *only* great-granddaughter," Isabel reminded him, laughing.

Sam could see that there was a special bond between Isabel and her great-grandfather. It hadn't been obvious when there were other people around. But now it was clear to Sam that Isabel and her great-grandfather meant a great deal to each other.

Isabel doesn't have a thing to worry about, thought Sam. *This interview is going to be great!*

"Okay, let's start," Isabel told her great-grandfather. "I've been hearing about a charm our family used to own. A golden dog. Is it true that Great-uncle Will liked to play with it?"

At the mention of Will and the golden dog, Mr. Ottinger frowned. "I don't want to talk about that," he said sharply.

In a matter of a few seconds, he seemed to be shutting down completely.

Isabel's smile faltered. "But . . . why not?"

"This business of the past . . ." Mr. Ottinger fingered the carved dragon's head of his cane. "It was difficult enough living through some of it *once*. Why stir up all those memories again?"

Sam took her camera from her backpack, removed the lens cover, and checked the settings. She didn't want to interrupt, but she wondered about the sudden change that had come over him. It was as if the memories of Will and the golden dog were simply too painful to talk about.

"You're always talking about how important family is," Isabel said. "Well, I want to know more about mine."

"*I'll* decide what's important for you to know about this family," Mr. Ottinger said, with an impatient wave of his hand.

"But, Great-grandpa . . ."—Isabel let out a sigh of frustration—". . . you promised to give me a good interview!"

Mr. Ottinger stared stubbornly, silently, in front of him.

So much for having a great interview, thought Sam.

At that moment, Wishbone appeared from beneath the rose trellises in Mr. Ottinger's garden with two sticks in his mouth. He had managed to drag them from a pile of branches that had been trimmed from the hedges—just one of the many treasures he had come across.

Letting the sticks drop to the ground, Wishbone rolled in the soft dirt at the edge of the path. Ahead of him was the fountain, with its three dolphins spouting streams of water. Paths led away from the fountain in several different directions.

Wishbone cocked his head to one side, looking at a small path at the far side of the fountain, marked by two dogwood trees. He hadn't explored that one yet. "But I guess I should save something to do with Iggy and Axel after I get to know them better. . . ."

As Wishbone trotted back toward the house, his sharp nose picked up the scent of something meaty and delicious. Wishbone spotted a doorway set into the rear wall of the house, just past the terrace. The door was propped open with a chair, and the tasty smells of roast beef and potatoes wafted out.

"Mmm-mmm! With any luck, I'll find Iggy and Axel inside. Then I can give them lesson number two: begging for scraps with proper canine charm and manners."

Running over to the doorway, Wishbone ran through it and found himself inside a large, sunny kitchen. Isabel's German shepherds were nowhere in sight, but Wishbone saw the heavyset woman he had seen on the terrace earlier. She was standing in front of an open oven. Upon seeing Wishbone, she grabbed a broom that was leaning against the wall.

"Where did you come from?" she called out sharply.

Wishbone gave the woman his best smile. "Is that roast beef I smell? I'll be happy to help you get rid of any leftovers— Hey! Watch it with that broom!"

Wishbone jumped as the woman swatted at him, shooing him toward the door. "Out! We can't have strays in here!" she scolded.

"I'm *not* a stray!" Wishbone was insulted. He then noticed Iggy and Axel standing in the open doorway. "Just the dogs I was searching for! Look, I know we got off to a bad start yesterday. But Isabel mentioned that you guys needed some training, and I thought we could try lesson number one again—"

The German shepherds leaped toward Wishbone, growling and barking.

"Yikes! I take it that means you're not interested in lesson one, so let's skip straight ahead to lesson three: When in doubt . . . *run!*"

Wishbone twisted around the broom and ran in between the large woman's legs. Seeing an open doorway, he raced through it.

"Come back!" the woman called.

"Right in the middle of a valuable lesson in canine behavior? Not a chance!" Wishbone ran down a long hallway. He hoped Iggy and Axel appreciated what he was trying to show them, but their angry barking made him doubt it. The deafening sounds echoed all around Wishbone.

The terrier heard a door open close by.

Wishbone caught a glimpse of Sam, Isabel, and Isabel's great-grandfather as he raced past the doorway. "Sorry, guys. No time to explain!"

Breathless, Wishbone raced toward a wide staircase that curved upward. His nails scraped at the carpeting as he scampered up one flight, then another. Glancing behind him, he saw that Iggy, Axel, the heavyset woman, Sam, Isabel, *and* Isabel's great-grandfather were all coming after him, in hot pursuit.

"Yikes!" Wishbone was panting, but he didn't stop.

He ran up one final staircase—and found an open door leading into a dim attic filled with shelves, boxes, trunks, and racks of clothing covered with dusty plastic sheeting.

"Looks like this is the end of the line. . . . Ahh—ahh-choo!" Wishbone's paws had stirred up a cloud of dust that sent him into a fit of sneezing. "Ahh-choo! Ahh-choo! Ahh-choo!"

The force of it sent Wishbone sideways—past a rack of old dresses and into a pile of cardboard boxes that came tumbling down on him.

"He-elp!" Wishbone covered his muzzle with his front paws. When he looked again a moment later, he saw boxes scattered all around him. Some of them had opened, and photographs and papers spilled out onto the dusty floor.

Iggy and Axel were just leaping up the last flight of stairs. Their barks echoed off the bare walls and ceiling beams. Behind the German shepherds were Isabel, Sam, the heavyset woman, and Mr. Ottinger.

They were closing in on Wishbone. And they all looked very displeased.

Chapter Nine

Wishbone backed slowly away from Iggy and Axel, but the boxes prevented him from moving more than a few inches in any direction.

"Look what you've done, Wishbone!" Sam scolded.

"I can explain. . . ." Wishbone gave a guilty wag of his tail—then stiffened when Iggy and Axel started barking again.

Isabel grabbed both German shepherds by their collars and pulled them back toward the stairs. "Down, boys!" she said sternly, but the two dogs continued to strain against her hold. "Mrs. Hazlett, could you please take Iggy and Axel outside?"

As soon as the two shepherds and Mrs. Hazlett were out of sight, Mr. Ottinger pointed his cane at Wishbone and asked, "How did he get in here?"

"Wishbone?" Sam asked. Pushing aside the rack of clothing, Sam started toward him.

Wishbone gave a friendly bark as he launched into his story. "You see, I thought I'd help Isabel train Iggy and—"

"Wow! Take a look at these!" Isabel exclaimed.

Wishbone saw that she had bent over some yellowed papers and old photographs that had spilled from one of the cardboard boxes. "I've looked through some old clothes and books and stuff up here before"—she gestured toward the rack of dresses Sam had just moved—"but this is the first time I've seen these photos."

Picking up one of the photographs, she showed it to her great-grandfather. "Isn't that the gazebo that's in the back gardens? Is he a relative of ours?"

As Mr. Ottinger leaned forward to see the photograph, Wishbone looked, too. It showed a young boy sitting on a grassy lawn next to an open structure with carved wooden columns and a fancy roof. All around him were flowers and leafy trees that made Wishbone itch to be outdoors.

Mr. Ottinger stared at the soft-brown-colored photograph for a long time without saying anything. The expression in his eyes grew sad. Finally, he shook himself and said gruffly, "That's your great-uncle."

Wishbone saw the meaningful looks that Sam and Isabel shot at each other. "You mean Will?" Isabel asked.

Her great-grandfather gave a quick nod and then turned away from the photograph.

"Look at what he's holding!" Isabel said, pointing at the photograph. "Great-grandpa, is that the golden dog?"

"Dog? Where?" Wishbone wagged his tail and looked more closely. Sure enough, there was a glistening charm in the boy's hands. The image in the photograph was small, but Wishbone could make out the shape of a dog. "So that's the mysterious golden dog. You never found out what happened to it?"

The terrier looked expectantly at Mr. Ottinger. The old man stared stubbornly into the shadows of the attic without answering.

"Uh . . . never mind, Great-grandpa," Isabel said.

Wishbone could see the disappointment in her face.

Putting the photograph down, Isabel picked up another and held it out so Mr. Ottinger had no choice but to look at it. "What about this one?"

The old man cleared his throat and blinked a few times. As he took the second photograph in his hand, Wishbone caught a glimpse of it. A boy and a young man stood next to a horse-drawn sleigh. Sunlight glinted off high drifts of snow.

"Well, now. . . . That's my father and me, after the annual winter race," Mr. Ottinger said, chuckling to himself. "I do believe that was the year Lee Johnstone's horse got spooked. Ran his sleigh clear through the Trumbulls' barn and came out the other side, with half a dozen squawking chickens clinging to him."

"I never heard anyone tell that story before," Isabel said, laughing.

"Wasn't Lee Johnstone related to Moses Johnstone, the founder of Oakdale?" Sam asked. "One of his relatives is in our class, Isabel. Hank Dutton."

Mr. Ottinger nodded. "The Johnstones and the Ottingers both go way back in Oakdale," he said. "I'll never forget the time Lee Johnstone and I . . ."

As the old man talked, Wishbone sat back on his haunches to listen. "Keep talking, big guy. There's nothing I like more than a good story!"

"Your great-grandfather is an amazing storyteller," Sam said, as she, Isabel, and Wishbone went down the attic stairs a while later. "I think I got some great pictures for the article."

For the past hour, Sam, Isabel, and Wishbone had listened to Mr. Ottinger talk about what Oakdale was like when he was young. He had sat on a cardboard box, telling story after story, as Isabel asked him about photographs from the box Wishbone had accidentally knocked over.

"I think the article's going to be great, but—" Isabel walked ahead of Sam, lugging the box of photographs and letters. Sam couldn't see her face, but her voice didn't sound completely happy. "I just wish I could have gotten Great-grandpa to talk about Will and the golden dog."

She pushed through a doorway leading into her bedroom. It was large and airy, Sam saw, with flowered wallpaper, a window seat, and a canopy bed.

As Isabel set the box down on her braided rug, she let out a sigh. "I keep thinking we're getting closer. But no matter how hard I try, there's always something that holds him back."

"It seems to happen whenever Will's name comes up," Sam said. She placed her camera on the window seat, then sat on the edge of Isabel's bed. "Maybe the memories are just too painful for him."

"That's why I keep trying to get him to talk about Will," said Isabel. "He keeps all of his sadness bottled up inside."

"There must be *something* we can do to help," Sam said.

"That's what I keep thinking!" Isabel said excitedly. "That's why I really want to find—"

She stopped herself in mid-sentence.

"Never mind," Isabel said.

Sam wondered what Isabel had been about to say—and why she had decided not to finish her thought.

"Anyway, we got a great interview for the school

paper," Sam said. "Thanks for knocking over that box of photos, Wishbone." She glanced over at him, as he sat on the floor next to the bed. "I guess we can't be too upset with you for sending us on that wild chase."

Wishbone barked and wagged his tail, as if to say "Glad to be of service!"

"Isabel, Wishbone and I better get going," Sam said. "Joe must be wondering where Wishbone is."

As Sam stood up, a book on Isabel's bedside table caught her eye. Its leather cover was worn and faded, but Sam saw the image of a merry-go-round in faded yellows, reds, and blues. Something was written below it in a childlike script, but Sam couldn't make out the words.

"What's this?" she asked, picking up the book.

Before she could open the cover, Isabel snatched the book away from her. "Don't look at that!" Isabel said. She must have seen how surprised Sam was by her harsh reaction, because she quickly added, "It's . . . uh . . . very delicate."

"Sorry," said Sam. "I didn't know." She *had* handled the book carefully.

Isabel returned the book to her bedside table, then gave Sam a nervous smile. "I think your backpack is still in the library. We can get it on your way out."

Sam had the sudden feeling that Isabel wanted her to leave, and she got the impression that Isabel was hiding something from her.

Don't be so dramatic, Sam finally told herself. But as she, Isabel, and Wishbone went downstairs and got her backpack, she couldn't shake the feeling that something strange was going on.

Sam and Wishbone were just about to leave the big house when Isabel's mother came in the front door. "Hello, darling," Mrs. St. Clair said. After kissing Isabel on the cheek, she turned to Sam. "How nice to see you again. Isabel was so excited after the newspaper meeting yesterday. Thank you for suggesting that she get involved with the project."

"But . . ."—Sam looked at Isabel's mother in total confusion—". . . Isabel wasn't *at* the mee——"

Before Sam could finish, Isabel gasped and said, "Oh, my gosh! It's almost dinner time! Your dad's going to wonder where you are, Sam."

Sam felt herself being herded toward the front door. She barely had time to say good-bye before she and Wishbone found themselves outside. For a moment, all Sam could do was stare at the front door that had closed so abruptly behind her.

"What was *that* all about?" she said under her breath to Wishbone. As she got her bike, Sam was more confused than ever.

Isabel had told her, Joe, and David that she was out of school sick the day before. But Mrs. St. Clair had made it clear that Isabel had told her that she was at school. Sam knew for a fact Isabel hadn't been at school. But . . .

"Why would she lie?" Sam wondered aloud. Wishbone gazed at her with warm, friendly eyes. As Sam reached down to pet him, another question sprang to her mind.

"Tell me something, Wishbone," she said. "If Isabel wasn't home sick, and she wasn't at school . . . then where *was* she?"

Chapter Ten

Wishbone wondered about Isabel as he ran alongside Sam's bike, heading back toward the Talbots' house. "Tell me something, Sam," he called out. "Why would Isabel lie about where she was Tuesday?"

Sam seemed to be mulling over the same question. And, judging by the troubled look on her face, she hadn't come up with an answer.

Wishbone barked happily when he caught sight of Joe and David playing basketball in Joe's driveway a short while later. "Hi, guys! Maybe you can help us figure this out. . . ."

"Joe! David! I'm glad you're both here," Sam said, as she stopped her bike. "Something really weird just happened at Isabel's house."

"Sounds serious," Joe said, tucking his basketball under his arm.

Wishbone listened while Sam told Joe and David about what just happened.

"You mean, Isabel lied to her mother about being at school? *And* she lied to us when she said she was home sick?" David said when Sam was finished telling her story.

Sam nodded. "I keep wondering why she would lie. I mean, where could she have been that she couldn't tell us or her mom?"

"Taking her dogs to obedience school?" Wishbone suggested. "They sure could use it."

"I don't see the point of lying," Sam added.

"I don't get it, either," Joe said.

"We don't really know her very well yet," David pointed out. "And she kept something from us once before. She didn't tell us she was related to Mr. Ottinger, remember?"

"But she explained that. I bet she can explain this other business, too," Joe said. "I mean, what could Isabel possibly have to hide? The only mystery to be solved is finding out who took the model engine. And I seriously doubt Isabel is involved."

Wishbone barked and rolled in the grass next to his friends. "Good point, Joe. Damont is our number-one suspect there, right, guys?"

"It does seem unlikely," Sam admitted. "Isabel is just as convinced as we are that Damont did it. But you have to admit, the timing is weird. The very morning the engine was taken, Isabel wasn't at home *or* at school. I agree it doesn't make sense that she would steal something that already belongs to her family. But we have to consider everything that's even the least bit suspicious. That's what Sergeant Cuff does in *The Moonstone.*"

Wishbone's ears perked up at the mention of the classic mystery. "Quite right, Sam!"

"Sergeant Cuff's investigation takes a lot of twists and turns, but at one point he even suspects that the owner of the diamond is the thief," Sam explained. "On the surface, it doesn't make sense, but Sergeant Cuff considers the possibility because of Rachel's suspicious behavior."

Joe tossed his basketball from hand to hand as he listened. "That *is* like Isabel," he said. "But I still don't think she took the model engine. I'm sure she can explain everything—if we give her a chance."

Wishbone thought over his buddy's words. "I hope you're right, Joe. But there's something about Isabel I just don't trust. . . ."

As Sam listened to Joe's arguments, she began to wonder if she was being too hard on Isabel. "You're right, Joe. Maybe I'm just being extra-suspicious because we haven't found the model engine yet. There could be a good reason Isabel lied to us."

In her mind, Sam replayed some of the afternoon's events. Isabel had been so sensitive about the old book Sam had picked up. Sam couldn't imagine what that might have to do with the missing engine, but . . .

"I guess I should at least give Isabel a chance to explain," Sam said. "Joe, would it be okay if I use your phone to call her?"

"Sure," he answered.

Sam, David, and Wishbone followed Joe inside, and Sam used the portable phone in the living room. Mrs. St. Clair answered after two rings, and Sam asked to speak with Isabel.

"I'm afraid you just missed her," Isabel's mother told her. "She went to Jackson Park to meet a boy from school."

"Really?" said Sam. Isabel hadn't said anything to her about meeting someone. "Did she say who?"

"Damont Jones," Mrs. St. Clair responded back over the line. "I believe that was his name."

Sam frowned. After thanking Isabel's mother, she hung up. "Isabel's going to Jackson Park . . . to meet Damont."

"Why would she get together with him?" David asked. "Do you think they worked as a team to steal the model engine?"

"I still say it doesn't make sense," Joe said.

"There's one way to find out," Sam said, with a strong feeling. "Let's go find them. I wanted to talk to Damont some more, anyway, about the paint I saw on his shirt. Maybe we can clear up everything all at once."

David and Joe looked at each other and nodded. "Let's go," Joe agreed.

Wishbone trotted over to the boys, barking and wagging his tail.

"Come on, Wishbone," Joe said.

A few minutes later they were on their way. The late afternoon sun was low in the sky, and the spring breeze was growing cooler. As they approached the park on their bikes, Sam scanned the trees, paths, and grassy lawns, looking for Damont and Isabel.

"There!" said David.

Sam slowed her bike and glanced in the direction David pointed. At first all she saw were some joggers and a few kids playing ball. Then she caught sight of a boy and a girl walking toward the other side of the park on one of the paths. Just before they disappeared behind a tree-covered hill, the boy turned in their direction, and Sam got a clear look at his face.

"It's them, all right," Sam said. "Come on!"

Sam, Joe, and David rode into the park, with Wishbone running alongside. As Sam started down the path

Isabel and Damont had taken, she pedaled as fast as she could. Sam was breathless when she, Joe, and David reached the tree-covered hill a few minutes later.

Just in front of her, the path forked. One direction led farther into the woods. The other curved past a maintenance shed and circled back toward the street. Sam didn't see Isabel and Damont in either direction.

"Great," she said, disappointed. "Which way, you guys?"

Joe and David both shrugged, and they had a hard time trying to catch their breath. Joe finally said, "Why don't we try—" He broke off as Wishbone started barking. "What's the matter, boy?"

Wishbone faced the maintenance shed and kept barking. Sam hadn't really paid attention to the shed until that moment. Now that she looked more closely, she saw that the door was wide open. "Is someone in there, Wishbone?" she asked.

Wishbone trotted closer and barked again.

Shooting a glance at Joe and David, Sam rode over to the shed. "Damont? Isabel?" she called out.

Joe and David were right behind her. "Is anyone in there?" David asked.

Sam peeked inside. The windowless shed smelled of earth and grass. Sam spotted the shadowy shapes of a lawn mower and some rakes, but the corners of the shed were in total darkness.

"Come on, guys." Sam took a deep breath and then stepped inside. She heard Wishbone's nails click on the concrete floor as the terrier followed David and Joe. "Let's check the corners before we—"

Sam heard footsteps just outside the door.

"Hey!" she called out. "Who . . . ?"

Before she could finish her question, the door to the

shed slammed shut, leaving Sam, Joe, David, and Wishbone in total darkness.

"The door!" Joe called out.

Sam whirled around and felt with her hands until she found the door. She pushed with all her strength, but the door didn't budge.

"We're locked in!" she said.

Chapter Eleven

Wishbone scratched at the inside of the door, barking loudly. "Let us out! Is anyone out there?"

His supersensitive ears picked up the sounds of sneakers in the grass outside the maintenance shed. It was the same sound that had caught his attention when he first saw the shed. But instead of coming closer, the sneakers ran away from the shed.

"Hear that? Someone's running away," said Joe.

Wishbone couldn't see his best buddy's face in the darkness, but he heard the angry tone in Joe's voice.

Wishbone scratched at the door, barking even louder while Sam, Joe, and David continued to call for help.

Within moments, the door suddenly swung open. Wishbone blinked as his eyes adjusted to the burst of light that flooded the shed.

"What's all that noise?" a stern voice spoke up right in front of Wishbone.

Looking up, Wishbone saw a man who was wearing blue overalls and work gloves. He was holding a rake—and looking at Joe, Sam, David, and Wishbone with disapproving eyes.

"Don't you know this is town property?" the man said. "What are you doing in this shed?"

"We were locked in," Sam said, as she, Joe, and David followed Wishbone out of the shed. "Did you see anyone running away from here a second ago?"

"I haven't seen anyone at all—except you three." The man looked as if he wasn't sure he believed them. "You shouldn't have been in the shed in the first place." The man tapped a metal plaque nailed to the outside of the door. "Like the sign says, 'Keep Out.'"

"Sorry. I guess we didn't see it. The door was wide open, and we thought someone was in here," David explained.

Sam and Joe also apologized. Then they walked away from the shed, with Wishbone trotting alongside. As the three friends got back on their bikes, they glanced up and down the paths that forked around the shed.

"Are you guys wondering the same thing I am?" Sam asked. "Did Damont and Isabel just lock us in that shed?"

"Correction, guys." Wishbone wagged his tail and gazed up at his friends. "I heard only *one* pair of sneakers, so it had to be Damont or Isabel."

David shrugged and said, "They were walking this way, but . . . Why would they do it?"

"I repeat, it was only one person." Wishbone barked, then sighed when the others ignored him. "No one ever listens to the dog."

"I still don't buy it," Joe said. "Isabel acts like she really wants to get the model engine back."

"All I know is that she's acting really strange," Sam said with a shrug. "I'm going to talk to her and Damont as soon as I can, and find out what they've been up to."

"That's a good idea, Sam!" Wishbone barked out his approval. But his keen canine senses told him that talking to Isabel might not be so easy. Something about her was as sneaky as a cat.

Sam headed straight for Isabel's locker when she got to school Thursday morning. As soon as she rounded a corner in the hall, she caught sight of Isabel. She was standing next to her locker—and Damont was there with her.

"Again?" Sam hesitated, looking at the two. She could hardly believe her eyes, but Isabel and Damont were laughing and talking together like old buddies.

What's going on? Sam wondered. *When I told Isabel about the brown paint on Damont's shirt, she said she was sure he took her family's model engine. Now she's acting like they are best friends.*

Sam took a deep breath and walked toward them. As she approached, she saw Damont take two red bandannas from his backpack.

"We can use these for our costumes on Saturday," he told Isabel. "I thought we'd go as—"

"Hi, Isabel. Hi, Damont," Sam said as she came up to them. "Are you two going to the costume party together?"

Isabel glanced at Sam, then looked away uncomfortably. "I . . . uh . . ."

"Sure," Damont told Sam. With a smirk, he held up the bandannas. "I figure we'll make perfect outlaws."

"Why's that, Damont? Have you been practicing by breaking the law lately?" Sam asked.

Damont's eyes narrowed the slightest bit. "W-what are you talking about?"

Sam took a deep breath. She'd been wanting to talk to him again. Now she finally had her chance. "You know about the model engine that was stolen from Pepper Pete's," she said. "Whoever took it touched some wet brown paint that was used to make a repair on the railway—and that paint just happens to match the brown spot I saw on your shirt Tuesday."

Damont backed up a few steps, shaking his head. "Oh, no, you don't," he said. "You're not going to pin that on me. I didn't take the model engine."

He spoke so convincingly that Sam wanted to believe him. But the evidence still seemed to point directly at Damont. "What about the brown paint on your shirt?" she asked. "If you weren't in Pepper Pete's the morning of the theft, then where were you? Why were you late to school?"

A nervous glimmer came into Damont's eyes. Then it was gone, replaced by the smug smile Sam knew so well. "You've got it all wrong, Sam," Damont said. "I didn't take that engine. But if you want to believe I did, go ahead and think that I did."

With that, Damont turned and walked down the hall.

"Whoa . . . !" Sam murmured, following him with her eyes. She wasn't sure what to make of their conversation. Damont had sounded sincere when he said he hadn't stolen the model engine. But he had avoided her questions at Pepper Pete's, and again just now. He was plainly hiding *something*. . . .

"Maybe he's telling the truth," Isabel said, her voice cutting into Sam's thoughts.

Sam turned to stare at Isabel. She'd been so caught up in confronting Damont that she'd almost forgotten she had questions for Isabel, too.

"Oh—I forgot to tell you earlier," Isabel said, before Sam had a chance to speak again. "Great-grandpa agreed to hold the costume party at our house. He had so much fun telling us those stories yesterday, he decided he'd go along with the idea."

"That's great," Sam said. "But I wanted to ask you—"

"My parents are meeting with Miss Gilmore and the other party organizers right now," Isabel went on. "They're going to go crazy getting everything ready for Saturday, but it will be worth the extra work."

Sam had too much else on her mind to think about the costume party. "What's going on between you and Damont, Isabel? Doesn't it bother you that he could be the person who stole the model engine? Why are you going to the costume party with him?"

Isabel's cheeks turned red, but all she said was, "He's not so bad. Anyway, we don't know for sure that he took the engine."

"I don't want to believe he took it, either," Sam said. "But I can't ignore the evidence that points to him." She took a deep breath before adding, "And to you, too."

Isabel's mouth dropped open. *"What?!"*

"Joe, David, and I saw you two together in Jackson Park yesterday. We tried to catch up to you so we could talk to you. Instead, we wound up getting locked inside a maintenance shed."

"You're kidding!" Isabel blinked as she realized what Sam was getting at. "You think *I* did that? No way!"

Isabel shook her head so insistently that Sam found herself believing the other girl. But Sam reminded herself that Isabel still had a lot of explaining to do.

"Then what were you guys up to in the park?" Sam asked.

Isabel looked away from Sam. "We were just talking," she said, but Sam noticed that the color in her cheeks reddened again.

"There's something else," Sam added. "I know you

weren't home sick on Tuesday. And you were not at school. You lied, and I thought we were supposed to be friends. What is going on, Isabel?"

Isabel started to grab books from her locker. Then she stopped and looked down at her feet. "I can't tell you," she finally said. Her voice was so low Sam could hardly hear her.

"Why not?" Sam asked.

"I just . . . can't, that's all," Isabel said.

Sam took a deep breath, then said, "We're talking about *Tuesday,* Isabel—the day the model engine was stolen. Are you really going to tell me you can't explain where you were?"

"I . . . I'm working on something," Isabel finally said. "It's a surprise for Great- . . ." She broke off, then added quickly, "I can't say any more than that. It's a secret."

"What kind of secret could be important enough to lie to your family and friends?" Sam asked.

Isabel's gaze flickered for a moment over the kids who hustled up and down the hallway. Finally, she turned back to Sam and said, "I'm not doing anything wrong. You have to believe me, Sam. Can you please just trust me and not ask any more questions?"

For a long, uncomfortable moment, the two girls stood there staring at each other. Isabel's eyes filled with tears, and Sam gently touched her shoulder. "Will you ever be able to tell us what's going on?" she asked.

"Yes," Isabel promised. "Soon . . . I hope."

"Well . . . okay," Sam told her. "I won't ask any more questions—for now."

Isabel let out her breath. "Thanks, Sam. It really means a lot to me," she said with a smile. "Are you ready to go to class?"

"Sure," Sam answered. "Let's go."

Sam really wanted to trust Isabel. Maybe Isabel's secret had something to do with the old book that she hadn't wanted Sam to see. Maybe it wasn't related to the missing engine in any way. Sam certainly hoped so.

But as they walked to their first class, she couldn't ignore the doubts that remained in her mind.

Chapter Twelve

"Okay, folks, I've had my morning nap. Now I'm ready to get to work." Wishbone trotted toward the outskirts of Oakdale Thursday afternoon, heading for Isabel's house. "There are dogs to tame, and mysteries to solve!"

Wishbone wasn't sure what kind of reception Iggy and Axel would give him today. Sooner or later those German shepherds would surely realize how charming Wishbone was—and how much they could learn from him.

"I just hope it's sooner, rather than later! I want to nose around to see if I can help Sam find out what Isabel is hiding. And the job will be much easier if the local dogs cooperate."

When Wishbone reached Isabel's house, he headed right for the huge backyard. He thought that would be the likeliest place to find Iggy and Axel. He didn't see them on the terrace, so he trotted out toward the gardens.

The freshly turned earth and spring flowers sparked his sense of adventure. He had already explored most of the gardens. But there was still one path he hadn't visited, on the far side of the fountain. Maybe he'd find Iggy and Axel there. . . .

Running past the dolphins, Wishbone found the two dogwood trees that marked the path. "Dogwood trees, eh? My congratulations to whoever planned this part of the garden."

He was just sniffing at some flowers, when a flash of movement farther down the path caught his eye. The flickering black tail and glowing green eyes set every fiber of Wishbone's body on edge. His entire body became rigid.

"Cat!"

He barked out a red alert, taking off after the feline. She raced through the flowerbeds that lined the path on both sides, heading for a wide, grassy enclosure at the path's end.

The cat ran through a gazebo, then shot out the other side and disappeared beneath a thick hedge.

"Good riddance!" Wishbone let out a triumphant bark. Then he stiffened all over again when he spotted several other sleek, feline figures lounging on the gazebo's wooden floor.

He ran toward them, barking. To his surprise, they didn't move an inch.

"Don't you guys know I'm a dog? Run!"

As Wishbone leaped toward the closest cat, he realized something wasn't quite right. These creatures didn't smell like cats. They smelled like the earth-filled pots Ellen used for indoor plants.

"Hey! You're not real. You're ceramic cats!"

Wishbone stopped barking and sniffed at the felines. Each one held a different pose. One was curled up, as if sleeping. Another looked as if it were stretching out after a nap. They looked so natural and lifelike that even he had been fooled for the briefest moment.

"Ears, tails, whiskers . . ." All the details were painted

very realistically. Yet, now that Wishbone looked more closely, he realized there was an opening at the top of each ceramic cat. They all had a weathered, chipped look that told Wishbone they had been around for quite some time.

Wishbone was still sniffing at the decorative cats when he smelled a human presence nearby. Looking around, he saw Mrs. Hazlett coming down the path toward him with a broom in her hand.

Wishbone gave her a big doggie smile. "Hi, there! Do you happen to know where I can find Iggy and Axel—"

"You again!" cried the housekeeper. "Go on, now . . . scat!" She ran after Wishbone, swatting at him with her broom.

"But I was hoping Iggy and Axel could tell me more about Isabel. . . ." Wishbone wanted to explain himself, but Mrs. Hazlett just wouldn't give him the chance. She kept swinging her broom at him until she had driven him all the way to the front yard and down the driveway.

The outing hadn't turned out at all as Wishbone had hoped it would. He hadn't been able to learn about Isabel or get anywhere with her dogs' training sessions. Not only that, but his best soup bone was still buried next to the terrace of the big old house, and he had no idea when he'd be able to retrieve it.

With a sigh, Wishbone headed for home. "I hope Sam's having better luck than I am."

Chapter Thirteen

"That's the last customer, Dad," Sam called out Thursday evening. She locked the door after a group of teenagers left the pizza parlor. Then she turned the sign hanging in the window to read "Closed."

"I still don't know why you bothered to stay, honey," said her father. He came from behind the counter to clear the plates from the table that had just been vacated. "We weren't that busy."

"I like to help out," Sam said. She started to put chairs on the tables so the floor could be mopped. "Besides, if I were at home, I'd just keep thinking about how strange Isabel and Damont have been acting . . . and how the model engine is still missing . . . and how we haven't been able to figure out who stole it. . . ." She let out a sigh, brushing her blond hair from her face. "It just makes me feel so frustrated and—"

"Hurt?" her father guessed.

Sam nodded. "I thought Isabel was really nice when I first met her. She really seemed to want to be friends, but . . . Well, if she's a friend, why won't she be honest with me?"

Sam recalled that a similar situation had come up in *The Moonstone*. The mystery of the diamond deeply affected the friendships among the characters in the book. Rachel Verinder and Franklin Blake fell in love. After the theft of the diamond, however, they didn't speak to each other for almost a year. Suspicion caused them to cut off all contact.

"Have you tried talking to Isabel?" Sam's father asked.

"Yes—a couple of times," Sam told him. "She insists she's not doing anything wrong. But she's being really secretive and she won't tell me what she is doing. It's driving me crazy!"

"Maybe you should try talking to her again," her dad suggested.

"Maybe. We're meeting after school tomorrow to develop the photos and go over the finished article about her great-grandfather for the school paper. I guess I could talk to her then. But . . ."—Sam frowned and reached for the next two chairs—". . . it's already Thursday, and Mr. Ottinger gave us only until Saturday to get the model engine back. I'll feel awful if we can't locate the engine and he takes the rest of the railway away."

Sam's father gazed at her with an expression Sam couldn't quite understand. Leaving the dirty dishes in a pile, he put an arm around her shoulders and said, "You know, honey, you're not responsible for the loss of the engine."

"I know," she said, "but—"

"I'm proud of the way you've jumped in to help find the model engine," her dad went on. "But give the police a chance to do their job. That's what they're here for. There's still hope that they'll find the engine. And if they don't, I'm prepared to deal with the consequences. Promise me you won't worry about it anymore, okay?"

Sam could see that her father wasn't going to take "no" for an answer. "All right," she agreed.

Sam's father picked up the pile of dirty dishes and carried them out to the kitchen in back.

As Sam finished turning up the chairs, she couldn't stop thinking about the model engine. If Damont had stolen it, Sam was going to have to come up with some solid evidence to prove it. But what?

Sam looked slowly around the restaurant. There had to be something she was missing, some clue she had overlooked. If only she could—

"Hey . . . wait a minute!" she said excitedly.

Her gaze had come to rest on the antique cash register that stood at one end of the counter. Wedged in next to the register was the folded paper that contained the answers to Wanda's history quiz.

Hurrying over to the cash register, Sam picked up the paper and tapped a finger against it. "Maybe there *is* a way to prove conclusively who's guilty," she said aloud. "I've got an idea. . . ."

Wishbone was curled up in a chair after dinner Thursday night when the phone rang.

"I'll get it," Joe called from the couch.

Wishbone watched lazily, his paws draped over his rubber bone. Joe picked up the portable phone from the coffee table and answered. "Hello," he said into the receiver. "Oh, hi, Sam. . . . What?"

As Joe listened, he became excited.

"That's a great idea! The quiz was printed in yesterday's paper, so I bet Miss Gilmore already has some people's answers," Joe said. "I'll ask her to go through them and meet us here first thing in the morning. . . . Maybe we can figure out who stole the model engine."

Wishbone became instantly alert at the mention of the model engine. "What's a great idea, Joe?"

"Okay. I'll see you then. . . ." Joe said. "'Bye."

As soon as Joe hung up, he called out, "Mom! We need to call Miss Gilmore right away."

Wishbone jumped down from his chair and trotted over to Joe. "What's going on, Joe? Talk to the dog!"

Ellen appeared in the kitchen doorway, a confused look on her face. "Why? What's the matter?"

"You and Miss Gilmore made up a new history quiz, right?" Joe asked.

Ellen nodded. "It appeared in yesterday's *Chronicle,*" she said. "We wanted to make sure whoever got a look at the old quiz wouldn't have an unfair advantage."

"Sam thought of something," Joe said. "She figured whoever stole the model engine also copied the answer key to the old quiz. What if the person tries to use those answers for the new quiz?"

"I see what you mean," Ellen said. "The person wouldn't have any way of knowing we changed the quiz. Wanda told me that the questions from the first and second puzzles are very similar. The thief could be easily fooled. So if we find someone who used the old answers, we might have our thief!"

"Great thinking!" Wishbone barked his approval.

"Wanda won't be announcing the winner until Saturday's costume party," Ellen went on. "But she must have received some answers by now. I'll call her right now and ask her to go over the ones she has."

Wishbone was excited about the possibility of finally learning the thief's identity. The next morning, he, Joe, and Ellen all woke up extra early. By the time the doorbell rang, they had already eaten, and Joe had his backpack ready to take to school.

"Hi, Joe. Hi, Wishbone," Sam greeted them when Joe opened the door. She looked curiously past Joe, into the living room. "Hi, Mrs. Talbot," she said, seeing Ellen reading the paper on the couch. "Is Miss Gilmore here yet?"

Wishbone barked as he caught sight of Wanda coming across the lawn toward the front door.

"Hi, everyone!" Wanda called out. She held a sheet of paper that looked as if it had been cut out of the newspaper. "You were right, Sam. Someone *did* use the answers to the old quiz!"

Wishbone saw the excited looks that Joe and Sam exchanged. "Who was it?" Sam asked, as they all went inside.

Wanda held out the quiz answers and pointed to the name written at the top of the sheet of paper. "Damont Jones," she answered.

Chapter Fourteen

Sam stared at Damont's name. "This *proves* that Damont was the person who sneaked into Pepper Pete's," she said. "We were right about him being the thief."

Thinking back, Sam remembered that Damont had been in Pepper Pete's when they realized Miss Gilmore had dropped the answer key. He saw Sam put the quiz next to the register, so he would have known where to look for it.

"You don't exactly sound thrilled, Sam," Joe said.

"I guess I'm not," Sam said, surprised at herself. "I mean, I'm glad we found out who stole the engine. But . . . well, I wish it had turned out to be someone else. Stealing is a serious crime, and this just doesn't sound like Damont."

"That's why you two should go talk to Damont right away." Joe's mother spoke up. "Maybe he'll talk to you."

Sam looked at Joe, and he nodded. "I'm sure we'll find him at school," he said. "Let's go. We can pick David up on the way."

"I'll call Isabel and tell her that she should meet us there," Sam said.

As the three friends headed toward school, Joe and Sam filled David in on what they'd learned.

"There's Isabel," David said, as they approached Sequoyah Middle School.

Sam saw Isabel standing next to the entrance, scanning the faces of the kids who arrived. When she saw Sam, David, and Joe, she hurried over. "Hi, guys. Don't look now, but Damont is right behind you. Are you *sure* he took the model engine?"

Turning around, Sam saw Damont walking about a dozen yards behind them. "Pretty sure," Sam said.

Isabel looked as if she didn't want to believe Damont had stolen the model engine. But Sam knew they had to pay attention to the evidence—and it pointed to Damont.

"Here goes," Sam said. "Damont, mind if we talk to you for a minute?"

"It's a free country," he said with a shrug.

"We know you sneaked into Pepper Pete's early Tuesday morning," Joe began. "You gave yourself away when you answered every question on the town history quiz wrong."

Damont stared at Joe. "Wrong? No way! I aced that quiz."

His face showed the same smug smile as always—until Sam explained that Miss Gilmore and Joe's mom had created a new quiz.

"She changed it because we knew that whoever sneaked into Pepper Pete's took a look at the answer key," Sam said. "And your answers matched the *old* answer key exactly."

Damont glanced nervously from face to face, but he said nothing.

"Why can't you just admit you stole the model engine?" Joe added. "Once we tell the police about what happened with the quiz, they're going to find out, anyway."

"Wait a minute . . ." Damont took a step back. "I already told you, Sam, I didn't steal it!"

Damont sounded convincing, again, but Sam needed proof. "Come on, Damont. The only way you could have seen the answer key was by sneaking into Pepper Pete's. Plus, there's the brown paint I saw on your sleeve—and the fact that you were late to school that morning."

He didn't say anything at first, but Sam noticed the uneasy look in his eyes. "Okay. So maybe I was inside Pepper Pete's that morning," he admitted.

Sam exchanged excited glances with David, Isabel, and Joe. Finally, they were getting somewhere.

"But I *didn't* steal the model engine!" Damont insisted.

"Excuse me?" David asked. He looked as surprised as Sam felt.

Damont took a deep breath and let it out slowly. "I wanted to take a look at the answer key to the history quiz," he said. "I saw Sam put it behind the counter, and I heard Miss Gilmore tell you guys there were going to be great prizes—"

"And you figured you would copy the answers so you would be guaranteed to win a prize," Joe guessed.

Damont nodded. "I didn't exactly think about it ahead of time. But then Tuesday morning, I saw you guys go into Pepper Pete's and I thought, why not try?" He turned a cocky smile toward Joe, Sam, and David. "You

never even turned around until I was already in the back hallway. I stayed back there until after you left, and then I copied the answers to the quiz."

Everything Damont had said made sense. But Sam had a feeling he wasn't telling them the whole story. "What about the brown paint on your shirt?" she asked. "You must have taken the engine."

"No way," Damont repeated. "Sure, I looked at it. I guess I got paint on my sleeve when I picked it up. But I didn't take it. When I left Pepper Pete's, the model engine was still there."

"I don't know . . ." David said, frowning. "What about the other day at Jackson Park? We followed you and Isabel to try to talk to you, and we wound up getting locked inside a maintenance shed. Do you expect us to believe you didn't have anything to do with that, either?"

Damont gave them a guilty look before answering. "That was me," he admitted. "I saw you when Isabel and I were walking in the park. I knew you guys were suspicious of me because Sam asked me about the paint on my shirt. I figured you were following me, so I decided to teach you a lesson."

"You were in on it, Isabel?" Sam asked. She turned to Isabel, but Isabel had a look of surprise on her face.

"She didn't know anything about it," Damont answered. "We were only hanging out because she called and asked me to go to the costume party with her. We met in Jackson Park to talk about it. Isabel was about to leave when I saw you. I doubled back and hid behind the maintenance shed to see what you were up to."

Sam stared at Isabel in surprise. "Going to the party with Damont was *your* idea?" she asked. Sam couldn't figure Isabel out. She'd pretended to be so sure that Damont had stolen the model engine when Sam told her about the paint on his sleeve. Then, the very same day, she asked him to go to the costume party with her. Sam tried to make sense of this, but she was totally confused.

"Isabel and I are going to make great outlaws," Damont said, grinning. "I knew it the minute I saw her sitting in Jackson Park after I sneaked out of Pepper Pete's. I figured anyone who would cut school just to read a book was a natural outlaw. . . ."

Sam barely heard the last part of what Damont had said. Turning to Isabel, she asked, "You were at Jackson Park Tuesday morning? But . . . *why?* And why wouldn't you tell me about it?"

For a long moment, Isabel fidgeted with the strap of her backpack. Her face got redder and redder. Finally, she said, "I . . . uh . . . just remembered something I have to do before my first class. We'll talk about this later, okay?"

Sam stared in amazement as Isabel dashed inside the school, leaving her, Joe, David, and Damont standing there.

"I'm outta here," Damont said. Then he, too, disappeared through the front doors.

"That was weird," Joe said, frowning. "I mean, what is Isabel hiding from us?"

"I don't know," Sam said. "And what about Damont? He sounded pretty convincing when he said he didn't steal the model engine, but—"

"It could have been just a well-rehearsed act," David finished. "And once again we ask ourselves, who stole the engine?"

Sam was frustrated. "We know who smudged the paint, but we're still not sure who the thief is," she said, letting out a sigh. "It's a lot like what happened in *The Moonstone.*"

"Really?" Joe asked.

Sam nodded. "Sergeant Cuff found out that the varnish was smudged by Franklin Blake. But Franklin swore he didn't steal the diamond. He was one of the people who was working hardest to get the Moonstone back."

"Talk about one mystery on top of another," Joe said, shaking his head. "Finding out who made the smudge doesn't begin to solve the theft of the diamond."

That was for sure, thought Sam. Both in *The Moonstone* and in the theft of the model engine, each revelation only seemed to raise more questions.

That afternoon, Wishbone trotted toward Sequoyah Middle School. "Joe? Sam? David?"

He was curious to find out what had happened when his friends had spoken to Damont. If only he could get hold of someone to tell him!

"Hmm . . . let's see . . ." The terrier knew Joe often stayed after school to play basketball. And Sam mentioned that she and Isabel would be working on the article about Mr. Ottinger for the school paper.

As Wishbone rounded the corner near the front of the school, he spotted two familiar black-and-brown German shepherds. They were sitting on the cement walkway outside the entrance, their leashes looped around one of the metal rungs of the bike rack.

"Hi, guys! Isabel actually managed to get leashes on you? You must be making *some* progress. . . ."

Upon seeing Wishbone, Iggy and Axel jumped to their feet. They strained against their leashes, barking at top volume.

"Then, again, maybe you're not. You two obviously still have a lot to learn." Wishbone hovered just beyond the reach of their leashes. "If you would just cut out this barking routine and listen. . . ."

He turned as the front doors flew open and Isabel ran out. "Iggy! Axel!" she called, a worried look on her face. "Leave Wishbone alone, you two. . . ."

As she started to walk toward her dogs, Wishbone made a run for the doors. "I'd like to stay and chat, but there's a mystery that needs solving!"

Just before the doors closed, he scooted through and into the school. "Yes! Now . . . if I can just find Joe, David, or Sam . . ."

Wishbone headed in the direction of the gym, taking in the smells of linoleum, paper, clothes, and—"What's that smell?"

A sour, chemical odor coming from one of the classrooms caused his nose to crinkle up. Sniffing again, Wishbone realized he knew that smell. It was the same scent he'd sniffed on photographs Sam had developed at school.

"Yoo-hoo! Sam! Are you in here?" Wishbone paused to look through the doorway. The small room held a few tables and some photographs tacked to a bulletin board. Another door inside the room was closed, and a red light glowed above it. Two backpacks rested on the floor next to the door.

Wishbone crossed the room toward the door, sniffing as he went. As he got closer, a new scent mixed with the chemical odor. It was musty and interesting and familiar . . . and it was coming from one of the backpacks.

Seeing that the pack was unzipped, Wishbone couldn't resist sticking his muzzle in and . . .

"Ahhh-choo!" The dry, moldy dust tickled his nose without any letup. *"Ah-choo! Ah-choo! Ah-choo!"*

Sam was just lifting her last photograph from the tray of fixing solution when she heard barking and sneezing outside the darkroom door. "Wishbone!" she said into the darkness. "Is that you?"

She quickly clipped the photograph to the drying line, then opened the door. Sure enough, Wishbone was on his side, rubbing his muzzle against Isabel's pack. Sam noticed that he'd emptied half the contents of Isabel's pack with his vigorous rubbing.

"What's the matter, boy?" Bending down, Sam started to gather up Isabel's belongings. "Easy does it, Wishbone. You're making a big mess—"

Sam stopped in mid-sentence. Her gaze fell upon an old leather-bound book on the floor. She recognized the faded image of a merry-go-round on the cover. It was the book she'd seen in Isabel's room!

Leaning forward, Sam saw the childlike handwriting on the cover. It read: "William Ottinger."

Sam felt her heart beating faster. Had this book belonged to Isabel's Great-uncle Will, the boy who had died all those years ago?

She had to find out. Carefully, Sam opened the cover and read what was on the first page:

This diary belongs to William Ottinger, age 8.

Wow! Sam thought. The book hadn't just belonged to Will—it was his diary! There were pages and pages of entries, all written in a child's handwriting. Sam started flipping through the yellowed pages, and they opened naturally to the page with the last entry. Someone had placed a folded paper there, as if to mark the spot.

"Let's take a look, Wishbone," Sam said in a low voice. He had stopped sneezing and was looking at the

diary as if he were just as interested in it as she was. Sam reached down to pet the dog, holding the diary steady with her other hand.

Sam began to read:

> May 30—I did something I shouldn't have today. I borrowed Mama's gold charm without asking. She and Papa say they must be there when I play with the golden dog, but they were out and I couldn't resist.

"The golden dog!" Sam whispered excitedly. Her eyes flew to the next words:

> When Mama didn't find it in her jewelry box, she was very upset. So was Papa. I didn't dare tell them what I'd done, so I hid the charm away. I'll put it back when Papa is calmer. But for now, my model engine holds the key. . . .

That was it. The rest of the diary was blank.

Wow! Sam thought. If that was the last time Will had written in his diary, he might have died soon after—probably before he could tell his parents where the golden dog was hidden.

Looking back at the top of the page, Sam read the diary entry a second time. This time, she found herself staring at the very last words: " '. . . my model engine holds the key. . . .' " She read the phrase aloud, mulling over the words.

Then, suddenly, it hit her: If the model engine was the key to finding the golden dog, *that* must be why it had been stolen!

Sam's mind was racing a mile a minute. Isabel was the only person Sam could think of who could have read

Will's diary and known about the model engine "holding the key." And Isabel had told Sam that her big secret was something for her great-grandfather. Maybe she was trying to locate the golden dog!

Sam had not considered Isabel as a *real* suspect because she could not figure out what reason Isabel could possibly have for taking the model engine. Now she had her answer.

Chapter Fifteen

Wishbone gazed curiously from the musty old book to Sam's face. Sam was so excited, and then she looked guilty. Jumping up onto all fours, Wishbone gave her sleeve a playful tug. "What's going on, Sam?"

Just then, Isabel came back into the room. "I finally got Iggy and Axel calmed down and—" She stopped suddenly and grimaced when she saw the faded leather-bound book in Sam's lap. "You took that from my pack!"

"I did," Wishbone said.

"Wishbone was playing with your backpack," Sam said. "I was putting everything back inside it when I noticed Will's diary." As she got to her feet, she held the worn, leather-bound volume out to Isabel. "I'm sorry I read the diary without your permission. It's not mine, and I had no right." Sam paused. "You've been looking for the golden dog, haven't you?"

Wishbone looked back and forth between Sam and Isabel. The two girls were staring at each other without talking. "Hellllooo!"

"I read all about how Will hid the golden dog," Sam continued. "And about the model engine holding the key. I never thought I'd say this, Isabel, but . . . I think *you* took the model engine."

"I didn't!" Isabel backed up slowly.

"Then why have you been acting so strangely? Why have you been lying?" Sam asked.

Wishbone gazed up at Isabel. Her dark eyes made a sweep around the room before landing on Sam. "I can't—"

"*Please* don't tell me you can't explain!" Sam cut in. "If you value our friendship at all, then tell me the truth."

For a long moment, Isabel just stared at Sam. "Okay," she said at last. She took a deep breath and let her words out slowly. "I have been trying to find the golden dog. I wanted it to be a surprise for Great-grandpa. That's why I didn't say anything."

"You could have told me about it before," Sam said.

"I wouldn't have mentioned a word to him—or anyone else."

"That's the truth, Isabel. My pal Sam is as loyal as any dog!" Wishbone barked out.

"I know, but . . ." Isabel took the leather-bound diary from Sam and gently held it in both hands. "Great-grandpa doesn't like to rely on anyone but himself. I wanted to show him I could do this on *my own*—the way *he* would have done if he were in my place."

She let out a deep sigh, brushing her hair from her face.

Isabel continued. "I just thought that if he could learn what happened to the golden dog, it might help him to finally get over Will's death. I wanted to find it myself, to help him."

Wishbone glanced up at Sam. As she listened, her expression softened.

"But I haven't been able to find the golden dog yet," Isabel said, frowning.

Sam looked thoughtfully at the diary. "It says in there that the model engine holds the key. Did you search the engine?"

"I never had a chance," Isabel answered. "I didn't find Great-uncle Will's diary until the day the model railway went on display at Pepper Pete's. After my parents and I got home, I took a pile of old books from the attic." Isabel tapped the diary cover, her eyes shining. "This was one of them. I put it in my pack to take to school the next day. I figured I would read it during lunch, but then I stopped at Jackson Park on my way to school, just to read a little . . ."

"And you lost track of time?" Sam guessed.

Wishbone gave an enthusiastic bark. "I get that way myself when I'm in Jackson Park."

"I'll say! I wound up reading the whole thing," Isabel explained. "That's why I missed school. When I finally got to the part about the golden dog and the model engine, I figured I could get the golden dog back. But when I went to Pepper Pete's to check out the engine . . ."

"It was already gone," Sam finished.

Isabel nodded. "Without it, there's no way I can find the gold charm."

As Wishbone listened to Isabel's story, he began to understand her better. "Finding the golden dog should certainly be a top priority, but . . ." He cocked his head to one side and gazed at her. "Did you have to *lie,* Isabel?"

Sam was wondering the same thing. "What about you and Damont?" she asked Isabel. "When you learned about the brown paint on his shirt, you told me you were sure he must have stolen the model engine. Then, the same day, you asked him to go to the costume party with you."

"That must have seemed pretty weird," Isabel admitted. "I was sure Damont stole the engine—at first. I wanted to talk to him on my own, to see what I could find out. But I didn't think he'd admit anything if I asked him straight out. I had to think of some excuse to get him to talk to me. That's why I asked him if he wanted to go to the party with me. And then, well . . ."—Isabel gave a tentative smile—". . . he seemed kind of nice. Once I got to know him a little, I had a hard time believing he could have stolen the engine."

Looking up, Wishbone saw the thoughtful expression on Sam's face. "I guess I can understand why you would want to find the golden dog by yourself. But why couldn't you be upfront?" Sam asked. "Was it worth letting Joe and David and me think you were up to something dishonest?"

Isabel shook her head. "I didn't realize you would see it that way. I'm really sorry, Sam—about lying, about keeping information from you . . . about everything." She bent down to place the old diary in her pack. Then she turned back to face Sam. "Can you forgive me?"

Even before Wishbone heard Sam's answer, he knew what it would be. After all, Sam wasn't the kind of person to give up on someone.

"Sure," Sam said. "And I promise not to interfere in your search for the golden dog, as long as *you* promise—"

"No more secrets!" Isabel said, laughing. "But actually . . . I was hoping we could work together—to get the model engine back, *and* to find the golden dog."

Sam grinned at Isabel. "Count me in!" she said.

"Me, too!" Wishbone jumped up and pawed Isabel's leg. "If there's a dog to be found, I want to be on the case."

"The trouble is, we're kind of out of leads," Isabel said. "I have no idea how to track down the model engine."

"I've been thinking about that," Sam said. "There are two things we could try—test Damont's story, *and* see if we can come up with any more clues. It's a long shot, but it worked for Sergeant Cuff in *The Moonstone*."

"What's that?" Isabel asked.

Wishbone's tail wagged as he recalled the mystery. "Listen up, Isabel. This is where things start to get really interesting!"

"Sergeant Cuff came to what seemed like a dead end in his investigation, so he decided to re-create all the events that took place before the Moonstone was stolen."

"And?" Isabel asked, her eyes wide.

"I didn't read that part of the book yet," Sam said. "The point is, maybe we could do the same thing. If we reenact everything we did the morning the model engine was stolen, maybe we'll uncover something important—some clue we may have overlooked." Raising an eyebrow at Isabel, Sam asked, "So, what do you think? Should we try it?"

"Yes!" Wishbone barked out. "Yes! Yes! Yes!"

Isabel nodded. "Okay. Let's do it."

Chapter Sixteen

"Okay . . . places, everyone!" Wishbone barked out to the small gathering of people who had come together at Pepper Pete's early Saturday morning.

Joe, Sam, and David were there, of course, as well as Sam's father and Damont. Wishbone saw that Isabel and her parents and great-grandfather were also standing by. So were Ellen and Wanda. They all lingered next to the counter, where Walter had set up a tray of doughnuts, along with coffee and juice.

"Looks like all the major players are here." Wishbone wagged his tail and glanced from face to face. "You can start reenacting the crime any time!"

"Damont doesn't exactly look happy to be here," David said in a low voice. He nodded toward the other end of the counter, where Damont stood by himself, frowning at the doughnut in his hand. "How'd you get him to come, Sam?"

"I feel bad for him," Sam said. "I mean, his part in this whole thing is pretty sneaky, and he has to replay it in front of all these people. He only agreed because I warned him he'd be more of a suspect if he *didn't* cooperate."

"Okay, everyone!" Sam's dad called out. "Let's get started."

"I can't wait to see what will happen!" Tail wagging, Wishbone sat down to watch. He saw that Ellen, Wanda, the St. Clairs, and Mr. Ottinger had taken seats at some tables and booths. Sam, Joe, David, Damont, and Mr. Kepler stood by, ready to play their parts.

"I brought this to use as a reference," Sam said, waving a black-and-white photograph in the air. "It's one of the photos I took of the railway right after David finished putting in the guardrail."

Holding the photograph in one hand, she went to the front door with Joe and David. Wishbone saw that everyone else was waiting and watching. Even Mr. Ottinger was looking on with interest. He kept a firm grip on the dragon's head of his cane. His alert eyes took in every detail.

"I remember we got right to work," David said. He took a piece of wood from the paper bag he held and started toward the railway at the back of the restaurant. "I'll pretend this is the guardrail I made. I took it to the platform and—"

"Wait a minute," Sam interrupted. She was a few steps behind David, staring at the photograph in her hand. "Something's not right. Where's the toolbox?"

"Toolbox?" Wishbone trotted over to Sam and gazed at the photograph. A bulky metal toolbox was clearly visible in the picture. It sat on the floor in front of the platform, with its top wide open.

"I remember that metal monster!" Wishbone said. He had bumped into the toolbox himself when the derailed train had forced him to dive under the platform. But when he looked beneath the platform now . . . "You're right, Sam. It's not there!"

"I remember Sam pulled the toolbox from under here so we'd have the tools for the repair," David said. His face appeared behind Wishbone as he bent to take a look—and then frowned. "It's gone."

Wishbone gazed up at the faces around him. "Here's where a reenactment can be really helpful! How about hearing from the people who were here *after* Joe, David, and Sam left?"

"What about you, Damont? Did you see that toolbox when you were here?" Sam asked.

Damont nodded. "You guys left it wide open by the platform, on the floor. I almost tripped over it when I went to look at the model railway," he said. "But that was *after* I copied the answers to the history quiz and got some potato chips."

Wishbone watched eagerly as Damont reenacted his part, starting in the back closet, where he'd hidden until Sam, David, and Joe had left. Then he came back through the double doors, stopped at the counter to copy the answers to the history quiz and take some chips, and then went to look at the model railway.

"I ran the model train for a while. Then I picked up the engine to look at it," Damont said. "That's when Mr. Kepler got here. I almost jumped out of my skin when I heard the door rattle. I dropped the engine back on the track and—"

"You *dropped* the engine?" Mr. Ottinger spoke up from the table where he, Isabel, and Isabel's parents were sitting. He was obviously unhappy to hear that his railway had been mistreated by Damont.

"Uh-oh, I know that look." Wishbone shot a warning glance at Damont. "Get ready to be poked by a dragon cane. . . ."

"I was worried about getting caught!" Damont said. "I made a run for the back closet and then waited for my chance to leave."

"This is where you come in, Walter!" Wishbone looked expectantly at Sam's father, who walked over to the front door.

"I got here around nine," Sam's father said. "The first thing I did was clear some space for the deliveries I was expecting. That's when I spilled the olive oil and cleaned it up."

"That's also when Damont sneaked out," Joe put in.

Walter nodded. "I guess about ten, maybe fifteen minutes passed before I noticed the model engine was gone."

"But . . . where could it have gone?" Isabel wondered aloud. "It couldn't have disappeared into thin air."

"All I know is that when I looked at the model railway, the engine wasn't there," Sam's father said. "I searched everywhere for it, but—"

"What about the toolbox?" Wishbone asked.

"Did you see the toolbox?" Sam asked, interrupting her father.

"I remember that I was really frantic, looking for the engine. . . ." Walter paused for a moment, rubbing his chin. "The toolbox *was* there, now that I think of it. I remember I pushed it *away* from the platform, so I could see better to search." He frowned, then snapped his fingers and hurried over to the counter. "Under the counter, I think! I remember I wanted to put it somewhere out of the customers' way."

Sam's father went behind the counter, then bent to look under it. A moment later, he straightened up with a grin on his face. "It's here!" he announced.

Wishbone trotted over and sniffed the bulky metal toolbox as Walter dragged it from behind the counter.

"Let's put it back where it was," Wanda called out from her booth. "Didn't you say it was open, Sam?"

Sam nodded. Her father placed the toolbox next to the platform. Then she opened the lid and—

"Oh, my gosh!" Sam's hand flew to her mouth as she stared into the toolbox.

Wishbone followed her gaze—then yelped in surprise. There, lying on its side in the toolbox, was the model engine.

Chapter Seventeen

Sam could hardly believe her eyes. "Look!" she said excitedly. Carefully picking up the antique engine, she held it out for everyone to see.

Surprised exclamations burst from everyone in the restaurant. Within seconds, Sam and her father were surrounded. Isabel, her parents, Mr. Ottinger, Miss Gilmore, David, Joe, his mom, and even Damont all crowded around with eager expressions on their faces.

"Amazing . . ." Wanda said, shaking her head. "You mean, the engine *wasn't* stolen? It was right here all along?"

"It must have been," Sam answered. As she thought back over Damont's role in the reenactment, something clicked in her mind. "Damont said he dropped the engine when he heard my dad arrive," she explained. "And the toolbox was still open, and right in front of the platform. . . ."

"The model engine must have fallen inside," David said. "When it hit the tray inside the box, the impact could have been enough to make the lid slam shut."

"*With* the model engine inside," Joe finished. "That's why you didn't notice it, Mr. Kepler."

Wishbone gave a bark, jumping around Sam's legs. He seemed as happy as she was to have finally found the model engine. But Sam knew a few other people in the restaurant who were probably even more excited than she was. . . .

"Here, Mr. Ottinger," she said, holding the model engine out to Isabel's great-grandfather. "This belongs to you."

Mr. Ottinger took the engine. For once, he seemed at a loss for words. He simply stared down at the gleaming black engine.

"What a relief to have the engine back," Isabel's mother said. "Especially now that we know about Will's diary." She slipped a hand around Isabel's shoulders, smiling at her.

When Isabel and her family had arrived at Pepper Pete's for the reenactment, Isabel told Sam that she had finally told her parents and great-grandfather about Will's diary and her search for the golden dog. Now, as Isabel gazed at the engine in her great-grandfather's hands, she looked as if she could hardly contain her anticipation.

"It's hard to believe that after all these years we might finally find the golden dog," Isabel's father said. He turned to Mr. Ottinger. "Well, Grandfather . . . ?"

Isabel's great-grandfather turned the model engine over slowly in his hands. Then he cleared his throat and said, "If it weren't for Isabel, we might never have learned what happened to the golden dog. Goodness knows, I never had the heart to look at Will's diary. I'm certainly glad she did." He held the model engine out to his great-granddaughter. "I think the honor of finding the charm should go to you."

Isabel took the engine. "Let's see," she murmured.

"Will wrote in his diary that the model engine holds the key. . . ." she said softly.

Sam leaned closer while Isabel turned the engine over, looking at it from every angle. She examined the metal wheels and the rest of the underside. She poked at the coal bin, pulled the various levers, and looked closely inside the engine's cabin.

"Hey . . . what about the coal bin!" Isabel whispered. Her fingers flew toward a small door in the driver's compartment of the engine. Sam held her breath as Isabel caught a corner of the door with a fingernail and nudged it open. . . .

"It's a key!" Isabel announced.

Then she turned the engine on its side and shook it hard. A moment later, a small brass key—tarnished with age—fell into her palm.

"Wow!" Sam said. "That must be the key Will wrote about in his diary. You found it!"

"Yes, but—" Isabel stared down at the key in her hand, her eyes filled with confusion. "What's it a key *to?*"

Glancing around the restaurant, Sam saw that everyone was staring blankly at the old key. "Mr. Ottinger, do you have any idea?" Sam asked.

Isabel's great-grandfather looked long and hard at the key. Then he shook his head and said, "It's been too long. I just don't know."

Sam could see the disappointment in the old man's eyes. She could practically feel the stubborn stiffness return to his face.

"Until we find the lock that the key belongs to," Joe said, nodding toward the key Isabel held, "the location of the golden dog remains a mystery."

"Tell me again, Joe. . . ." Wishbone trotted alongside Joe and Ellen as they walked toward Isabel's house Saturday evening. "What exactly is going to *happen* at this Oakdale History Month costume party, anyway?"

Wishbone saw that candles had been lit in every window of Isabel's house. They shed a warm glow over the towering oak trees and wide lawn. Women in long, ruffled dresses and men in old-fashioned suits and shirts with stiff-looking collars flocked toward the rear gardens. Joe, Ellen, and Wishbone were among them.

Ellen picked up the skirt of her long dress as she walked over the grass. "I'm sorry Isabel's family didn't find the golden dog charm," she said to Joe. "It certainly would have given special meaning to tonight's gala."

Joe gave a tug to the cap that was part of his old-fashioned train engineer's costume. "Yes, but—"

"Hey, Talbot," Damont interrupted. "How come Wishbone's not in costume?"

Glancing back over his haunches, Wishbone saw Damont a few steps behind them. Except for the red bandanna knotted around his neck, Damont wore all black—right down to his vest and gun belt, with two toy pistols in it.

Wishbone sighed. "Don't you recognize a turn-of-the-century dog when you see one? Notice the wooden chew toy." He batted the piece of wood Joe had clipped to his collar. "Anyone familiar with their canine history would know that plastic squeaky toys hadn't yet been invented back then."

Wishbone heard strains of country music coming from up ahead. And then he sniffed the air. . . . *"Mmm-mmm* . . . barbecued ribs! I'll save some for you, Joe!"

Kicking up his heels, the terrier ran toward the sprawling green lawn in back of the house. As he rounded the side of the house, he saw that gas lanterns had been set up all over the terrace and gardens. Men, women, and children danced, ate, or simply stood around socializing. Musicians were playing fiddle music on a wooden platform near the dolphin fountain. Wishbone trotted past them, following the scent of sizzling ribs to the barbecue pit, on the far side of the terrace.

"Don't forget to leave some of those ribs for the dog, folks. I'm—" Wishbone stopped short when he caught sight of Iggy and Axel, hovering near the barbecue pit. Both dogs growled as they bit at discarded ribs. Wishbone noticed that guests took care to give the German shepherds plenty of room to move. "I see you two need a refresher course on lesson two: begging for scraps with proper canine charm and manners. Let me show you how it's done. . . ."

Iggy and Axel stiffened when they saw him. Just when Wishbone was sure they were about to lunge at him, he caught sight of a black feline tail twisting behind one of the guests.

"Cat!" He barked the alarm, and Iggy and Axel chimed in. In a flash, they were all after the intruder. "The chase is on!"

Wishbone ran as fast as his legs would take him. His barks mingled with those of the German shepherds, echoing in the evening air.

"Wishbone!" Joe and Ellen both called out.

Wishbone kept running. He saw the cat race past the fountain in a black blur. Iggy circled around one side, while Wishbone and Axel took the other side. "You're finally getting the hang of lesson one: uniting against a common foe. Good going, guys!"

The three of them raced past the two dogwood trees, their claws tearing up dirt and flowers. Up ahead, Wishbone caught sight of the gazebo. Its columns and benches made a tangle of black shadows in the twilight. Wishbone spotted a flash of movement, and two glowing green eyes that stared back at him.

"You're not going to get away this time. . . ."

Wishbone leaped over one of the benches and—

"Whoa!" His paws caught on the edge of one of the ceramic cat urns. He landed on his side with a *thud!*, then flipped over in time to see the urn topple over next to him.

Crash!

Shards of pottery rained over Wishbone's nose and paws. Barking and doggie yelps echoed all around as Iggy and Axel leaped into the gazebo behind him and slipped on the broken bits.

"What's going on!" Isabel called out.

As Wishbone scrambled back onto all fours, he saw Isabel, Sam, David, Joe, and Ellen running toward the gazebo.

"What have you gotten into now, Wishbone?" Ellen asked.

"It wasn't my fault!" Wishbone tried to explain. "You see there was this cat, and— *Ouch!*"

Wishbone's scrambling paws hit something metallic. Looking down, he saw a square box half-covered by shards of the broken urn. He bent to sniff it, but he was stopped as Joe grabbed him by the collar.

"Gotcha!" Joe said. "You've caused enough trouble, Wish——"

"Look—a box!" Isabel exclaimed.

While David kept a tight hold on Iggy and Axel, Isabel bent down and brushed aside the bits of pottery covering the square metal piece Wishbone had stepped on. Sure enough, there was a small brass box. It was so tarnished with age that its surface was speckled with splotches of gold, brown, green, and black.

"Wow!" Sam said. "That looks as if it's been here forever. . . ."

Isabel stared at the box, then drew in her breath. "There's a keyhole! You don't think—"

"You think this could be the lock that Will's key fits into?" Joe asked.

"Why not?" Sam said. "Isabel, where's the key!"

"It's right here," Isabel said.

As Isabel reached for a chain at her neck, Wishbone saw the small brass key that hung from it. "Will's key!" He barked excitedly. "Try it, Isabel!"

Isabel removed the key from its chain. As she brought it closer to the keyhole, Wishbone grew more and more excited. Isabel slowly inserted the key into the lock and—

"Wow!" Isabel exclaimed. "It's a perfect fit!"

Chapter Eighteen

Wishbone jumped forward, pulling against Joe's tight grip. "Open it, Isabel!"

"It won't turn," Isabel said. She bit her lip as she fiddled with the key, twisting it first one way, then the other. Wishbone heard the scrape of metal against metal, and the hairs along his back stood up on end.

"Come on . . ." Sam said, her eyes on the box. "It *has* to work."

"Yes!" Isabel gave a victorious cry as the key turned in the lock with a metallic screech. Holding her breath, she tugged at the lid. It seemed to resist at first, but Isabel finally succeeded in opening it.

"Oh, my gosh!" Isabel stared wide-eyed into the box.

"What is it?" Wishbone asked, pawing Isabel's leg. "Show me!"

Isabel reached into the box and took out a gleaming gold charm. It was shaped like a dog and had sparkling green gems for eyes.

"Unbelievable!" Joe said. Letting go of Wishbone's collar, he took a step closer to Isabel and the golden dog. "After all these years . . . you found it!"

Wishbone gazed at the golden dog as his tail wagged wildly back and forth. "Now, *that's* a treasure worth waiting for!"

As Sam, David, Ellen, and Joe crowded around Isabel, the terrier trotted over to the edge of the gazebo. "Speaking of treasures . . ."

Wishbone barked to Iggy and Axel, who were still sniffing the broken pieces of ceramic. They both looked up at Wishbone, then ran over, barking.

Wishbone could still smell the cat, too, but . . . "I've got a better idea, guys. There's a bone near the terrace that's just waiting to be dug up."

To his surprise, the two German shepherds loped off in the direction of the house, playfully growling and nipping each other.

Wishbone gave a big smile as he followed behind. "There might be hope for you two yet."

Sam couldn't stop staring at the golden-dog charm. Even in the darkening twilight, highlights glistened off the sleek gold figure and twinkled from the dog's emerald eyes. The charm was beautiful—and valuable, no doubt. But Sam had a feeling its true worth couldn't be measured in dollars.

"Shouldn't we tell your family, Isabel?" she asked.

"Joe and I will go get them," Ellen offered.

Five minutes later, Isabel's parents and her great-grandfather hurried toward the gazebo, costumed in old-fashioned clothes. As Sam watched them, she could imagine that they had come to life from one of the old family photographs she had seen in Isabel's attic.

"Is it true?" Mr. St. Clair asked.

"You found the golden dog?" said Mrs. St. Clair.

Isabel's great-grandfather said nothing. As he used his cane to help him step into the gazebo, his eyes searched out the gold charm in Isabel's hand. He stopped in midstep. "The golden dog," he said softly. "I never imagined I'd see it again."

"Here, Great-grandpa," Isabel said, holding out the gold charm. "You've waited a long time for this."

Mr. Ottinger's face filled with emotion as he took the golden dog in his wrinkled hand. For a long time, he stared down at it. "But how . . . ?"

"It was in that cat urn," Isabel explained, pointing to the broken bits of pottery that littered the gazebo floor. "Will must have hidden it there. I guess he died before he had a chance to give it back. . . ."

Mr. Ottinger rubbed his fingers over the shiny surface. "Having this back again . . . it's like getting back part of Will's spirit. My, but that boy loved to play with this. He was like a mischievous puppy himself sometimes. . . ."

Isabel took her great-grandfather's hand and squeezed it.

As he looked down at her, tears filled his eyes, and he said, "This means a great deal to me, Isabel. But it's not nearly as valuable to me as you are. I'm a stubborn old man, and I'm too set in my ways. But I'm very, very happy that you and your parents have become a part of my life."

As Mr. Ottinger hugged Isabel close, Sam felt tears well up in her eyes. She was glad to see that the mystery of the golden dog had come to such a happy end. A smile spread across Sam's face as she looked at Isabel and her parents and great-grandfather exchanging laughs and hugs and exclamations of surprise.

I guess happy endings aren't just for books, she thought. *They can happen in real life, too.*

About Anne Capeci

Anne Capeci is a freelance writer who lives and works—and sometimes romps with the neighborhood dogs—in Brooklyn, New York. *Key to the Golden Dog* is the second book she has written for the WISHBONE Mysteries series; her first was *The Maltese Dog*. Anne has also written more than a dozen other mysteries for children and young adults.

Anne was drawn to Wilkie Collins's classic mystery, *The Moonstone*, for two reasons. Not only has it been called the first modern detective novel, but it also brings to life the rich atmosphere of London and the English countryside as they existed more than a hundred years ago. In writing *Key to the Golden Dog*, Anne wanted to portray Oakdale's unique past, so she created a secret from the town's early days that was linked to the modern-day mystery. As Wishbone, Sam, Joe, and David follow clues, they also discover an important missing piece of Oakdale's history. Anne likes to think that Wilkie Collins's celebrated detective, Sergeant Cuff, would have been proud of them.

In her spare time, Anne can usually be found with her husband, their two children, and their cat. She and her family have collected lots of old books, toys, tools, and antique glass bottles over the years, including some they found in their backyard. Anne has fun imagining the history each item might have had—dozens of mysteries that even Wishbone may not be able to solve so easily. . . .